"What do you think you're doing?" Joshua demanded.

"I had to take action before you sold the ranch," Honor said.

"No, you didn't. It's not your business!"

She glared at him. "It *is* my business. I could no sooner turn my back on this town than I could forsake my own family."

Joshua let out a scoffing sound. "You're affecting my future. And Violet's. How can you do that? Is this about getting even with me?"

She glared at him. "I'm not doing this for personal reasons."

Joshua narrowed his gaze. "So it has nothing to do with any feelings you might have for me?"

Honor sucked in a shocked breath and met his gaze head-on. "Everything I felt for you died the moment you lit the church on fire."

She could see the hurt in his eyes as he stormed out of the building. She felt bad about the animosity between them, but she couldn't allow her personal feelings for Joshua to sway her decisions.

If she did, Honor knew she would be in a world of trouble.

Belle Calhoune grew up in a small town in Massachusetts. Married to her college sweetheart, she is raising two lovely daughters in Connecticut. A dog lover, she has one mini poodle and a chocolate Lab. Writing for the Love Inspired line is a dream come true. Working at home in her pajamas is one of the best perks of the job. Belle enjoys summers in Cape Cod, traveling and reading.

Books by Belle Calhoune

Love Inspired

Alaskan Grooms

An Alaskan Wedding
Alaskan Reunion
A Match Made in Alaska
Reunited at Christmas
His Secret Alaskan Heiress
An Alaskan Christmas
Her Alaskan Cowboy

Reunited with the Sheriff
Forever Her Hero
Heart of a Soldier

Her Alaskan Cowboy

Belle Calhoune

LOVE INSPIRED BOOKS

Recycling programs
for this product may
not exist in your area.

ISBN-13: 978-1-335-50937-6

Her Alaskan Cowboy

www.Harlequin.com

Printed in U.S.A.

I will praise thee; for I am fearfully and
wonderfully made: marvellous are thy works;
and that my soul knoweth right well.
—*Psalms* 139:14

For my nieces—Celina, Kylie and Nina.
May you grow up to follow your hearts
and live out your dreams.

Chapter One

Honor Prescott sat on her white stallion and stared down from the mountain ridge at the sprawling Diamond R Ranch. From this vantage point, Honor had a bird's-eye view of the property. She could see horses in the paddock and a few ranch hands milling around. Snow from last night's snowfall covered the ground. She let out a sigh of appreciation at the vast acreage. This view had always been spectacular.

A few cars were parked in the driveway by the main house. She spotted Lee Jamison's distinctive yellow-and-tan wagon parked by the house. She felt her lips twitching at the sight of it. That van had to be older than Lee himself. As town attorney and a member of the town council, Lee was a beloved figure in Love, Alaska. Honor had come to the Diamond R Ranch today at Lee's request.

Honor drew her coat tighter around her as the February wind whipped relentlessly against her body. Although the sun was shining, there was a chill in the air. Honor grabbed Lola's reins and cantered toward the property. Riding her horse rather than driving over from the wildlife preserve was a luxury for her. Lately, she'd been so busy with work demands she rarely had the opportunity to spend time with her horse.

A feeling of nostalgia swept over her. It had been years since she had visited the ranch owned by Bud Ransom, the patriarch of the Ransom family. Bud had unexpectedly passed away a few days ago. She would miss him and his warm, solid presence. And she would be forever grateful to him for leaving the ranch to the town in his will.

Bittersweet memories washed over her as she surveyed the property. The two-story log cabin–style home was a generous size. It had been home for generations of Ransoms. Her ex-fiancé, Joshua Ransom, had grown up here with his grandparents, parents and his older brother, Theo. When they were dating, Honor had spent a lot of time at the Diamond R. Too much time, according to her own brothers—Boone, Liam and Cameron. They had been vehemently opposed to her relationship with Joshua, who had been in and out of trouble for the duration of their relationship. Joshua had been the ultimate rebel. Boone, who served as town sheriff, had hauled Joshua into his office on more occasions than she could count for a variety of charges. Drunk and disorderly. Vandalism.

But Honor and Joshua had been head over heels in love and committed to a life together. She had defended him at every turn, much to her family's dismay. In the end, their engagement had imploded after Joshua's involvement in a fire that had gutted a beloved town church and left a man seriously injured. It had been the final straw for her. Honor had given him back his diamond ring and headed off to college in Michigan. They hadn't spoken since.

After Honor had left Love, she'd discovered she was carrying Joshua's child. Weeks later she'd lost the baby. It still crushed her to remember how alone and scared she'd been. Since that time, Honor had turned to her faith and developed a relationship with God. She would never repeat the mistakes of the past.

Joshua had never known about their child. A few months after the miscarriage, she'd discovered that Joshua had gotten married. Joshua's quickie marriage mere months after their breakup had been a terrible blow to Honor's self-esteem. For some reason, it still stung.

Honor let out a sigh. The ranch represented a more innocent time in her life. She had experienced her first kiss in the barn. This ranch was where she'd fallen for Joshua. They had made plans for their future sitting amidst bales of hay. Their love had been genuine. Honor shivered as feelings of loss suddenly crept over her. After all this time, it still wasn't easy to think about losing the only man she'd ever loved. It had broken her young heart to end her engagement. She'd been so naive back then, believing that there might be a happily-ever-after for the two of them.

Joshua. Her first love and former fiancé. She hadn't thought about him in a very long time. Their relationship had ended in such a painful manner for Honor that it was easier now to stuff those memories deep down into a dark hole where they could no longer hurt her.

She had been a mere kid at the time—eighteen years old. What had she really known about love?

As she led Lola toward the stable so she could tether

her to a post while she met with Lee, Honor heard the crunching sound of footsteps walking on the snow. She swung her gaze up and found herself staring into the eyes of the last person she'd expected to see in all of Alaska.

Her heart constricted. Everything came to a standstill around her. The dark head of hair. The cleft in his chin. The sky blue eyes. Joshua Ransom, her high school sweetheart, was back in town. Her first instinct was to hop back onto Lola and ride off as quickly as possible in the opposite direction.

"Honor." The sound of her name tumbling off his lips was startling. It had been six years since she'd last heard it. Truthfully, she had never believed she would ever hear it again.

"Joshua." Somehow she managed to speak past the huge lump in her throat.

"It's been a long time," he said, his mouth quirking. "How are you?"

Her mouth felt as dry as cotton. "I'm doing well. And you?" she asked, marveling at the fact that they were able to exchange pleasantries despite the huge chasm between them.

"I can't complain. What brings you out here?" he asked, his eyebrows knitting together.

"Lee asked me to meet him out here. We understood none of the family was returning since Bud didn't want a service. When did you get back?"

"Yesterday. Theo and I flew in together from Anchorage."

Theo Ransom had moved away from Love years ago and joined the military. To her recollection, neither brother had been back to Love in the ensuing years.

"I'm guessing you didn't hire O'Rourke Charters to fly you here," Honor said. Her voice crackled with sarcasm.

A hint of a frown marred his brow. "No, we didn't."

She shouldn't have brought up the bad blood between him and the O'Rourke brothers—Declan and Finn. It harkened back to when she was dating Joshua and her own brothers had been staunchly against their relationship. There had been a lot of discord. It had all come to a head when she and Joshua had secretly gotten engaged and her family found out about it. Not a single person in town had been happy for them, except Bud. Despite his gruff demeanor, Bud had been a marshmallow at his center.

Joshua ran a hand over his face. "Bud never wanted a proper funeral, but Theo and I figured we should have some sort of memorial service for him. And we need to settle his affairs. Then I'll be heading home to Seattle."

Honor frowned. She hadn't heard a single word about a service for Bud. From what she had understood, Bud hadn't wanted any fanfare. The townsfolk would certainly want to know about the service so they could say a final farewell. Although she wanted to ask Joshua about Bud's desire to leave the Diamond R Ranch to the town of Love, she wasn't sure it was her place to ask Joshua probing questions. It would appear insensitive since his family was in mourning.

"I'm sorry about Bud. He was always kind to me."

Joshua nodded. "Thanks. He thought you were the real deal. I think he hoped you could straighten me up so I'd walk the straight and narrow path." Joshua let out a harsh-sounding laugh, although both he and

Honor knew he wasn't joking. Honor couldn't count on two hands the number of times Bud had pulled her aside and asked her to steer his grandson in the right direction. At the time, she had naively believed it was possible. Life had shown her how wrong she'd been to believe it. Being in love with Joshua had given her a pair of rose-colored glasses.

Honor smiled at the memory of Bud. "Well, he always saw the good in people. It was what he did best."

Joshua nodded. "He was a great man. I've always been proud to be his grandson." He grimaced. "I wish I'd been better," he muttered.

He didn't have to say any more. Honor knew exactly what Joshua meant. As a rebellious teenager, Joshua had been in and out of trouble so much it had broken his grandfather's heart and caused his family a world of embarrassment. He had tarnished the Ransom family name.

He jutted his chin toward Lola, then reached out and ran his palm across her side. "It's nice to see you and Lola are still a team."

Honor nuzzled her face against Lola's nose. "She's a part of me. Always will be. I'm glad Boone took care of her for me while I was away at school." Boone had paid for the costs of boarding Lola at a local stable, along with feed costs and her upkeep while Honor attended college and graduate school.

At the mention of her brother, Joshua's body seemed to stiffen. Honor couldn't help but think that after all these years the bad feelings still lingered.

As the small talk between them faltered, tension hung in the air. There were so many things left unsaid between the two of them, words they had never gotten the chance to say to one another. Honor opened her mouth, then shut it. What was the point? It was six years too late for closure.

Both of them had moved on with their lives. End of story.

She shifted from one foot to the other. "Well, I should go see to Lola," she said in a low voice. "Do you know where I can find Lee?"

"I saw him talking to Theo when I was out in the paddock. They were headed inside the house," Joshua said. For a moment he looked at her curiously. She imagined he was still wondering what she was doing here at the ranch. A gut instinct told her Joshua didn't know anything about Bud's bequest. The thought of his being blindsided made her stomach knot. Although she was fairly certain he had no interest in coming back permanently to Love, it still might rankle to learn his family's property had been given to the town he despised.

"Thanks," she said, lightly pulling at Lola's reins as she prepared to lead her toward the stable.

"Mr. Ransom!" a voice called out, interrupting the silence. Honor turned toward the house. Winnie Alden, housekeeper and cook for the Ransom family, was standing a few feet away from them with a crying baby in her arms. "I tried my best to settle her down, but she won't stop crying. I think she wants her daddy."

Winnie held out the child to Joshua. Honor's heart stilled. The little girl wrapped in the pink blanket was Joshua's daughter!

Joshua Ransom reached for Violet and held her against his chest. "Thanks, Winnie. I'll take it from here." He began to make rhythmic circles on Violet's back. Almost immediately, she quieted down.

"The baby whisperer strikes again," he said in a low voice next to his daughter's ear.

He swung his gaze toward Honor. She was staring at him with wide eyes.

"She's yours?" she asked in a shocked tone.

"Yes, she's mine. This is Violet," Joshua said, his voice filled with pride. "Violet Anne Ransom."

Honor's gaze locked onto Violet. She couldn't seem to look away from her. "She's beautiful," she said, darting a glance at his ring finger.

Joshua didn't hold it against her. It happened to him all the time. As a single father raising a little girl, he raised a lot of eyebrows. It was all right. Violet was his whole world.

He nestled her closer against him. "I should get her inside. It's pretty cold out here and her sweater is on the thin side."

"Go ahead. You don't want her to get sick," Honor said, her brow creased with concern.

Joshua sucked in a deep, steadying breath as he turned toward the house. He felt as if he'd been sucker punched. Although he had known it was a possibility to run into her during his stay in Love, he hadn't expected to see her at his family's ranch. And he wasn't quite sure what she was doing here. Her answer had been vague.

She was just as beautiful as she'd always been. Time had only enhanced her good looks. Her hair hung in glossy chestnut waves. Her cheekbones were more pronounced in her heart-shaped face. Now she was more woman than girl, one who exuded a great deal of confidence. It hadn't taken long for one of the locals to mention she was running a new wildlife center here in town. He felt a burst of pride knowing she had managed to achieve her goals.

She was no longer the eighteen-year-old who had dreamed of protecting animals and earning a degree in wildlife biology. Honor had reached out and successfully grabbed the brass ring.

It made him feel a little unsettled to know so much had changed since Honor had been his girl. In truth, it felt like another lifetime.

What did he expect? Time hadn't stood still. In many ways, Joshua felt thankful for the passage of time. It had given him the opportunity to change his life and circumstances. Over the past six years, he'd worked extremely hard to better himself. Redemption had been a huge motivating factor. He was no longer the selfish youth who had been impulsive and reckless. In his younger years, he had stolen a car to go joyriding, destroyed town property and been arrested for underage drinking and disorderly conduct. He had been a fixture at the sheriff's office. It had been easy for the residents of Love to believe he had been responsible for setting fire to the town's church and demolishing it. The townsfolk had already written him off well before the fire.

Joshua had made something of himself through sheer determination and grit. He had adopted Violet, the biological child of his ex-wife who had passed away shortly after Violet's birth. He had an impeccable professional reputation. His parents were extremely proud of the way he had pulled himself up by his bootstraps. And yet, he still yearned for the townsfolk of Love to think well of him. He still wanted their stamp of approval.

It had always bothered him that Honor's brothers had so thoroughly disapproved of him. He felt heat suffusing his neck as he remembered their vocal opposition to his relationship with Honor. Sheriff Boone Prescott had made it his mission in life to break them up and to catch his every misdeed. Joshua let out a sigh. To be fair, he'd enjoyed being a rebel. Until things had spiraled out of control and his whole life was in shreds.

Being in love with the sheriff's sister and the granddaughter of the town mayor, Jasper Prescott, had complicated matters. Law enforcement had not been on his side. Not that he'd made it easy on them. Joshua had been ornery and wild. He had deliberately pushed as many buttons as he could in his hometown and he'd never backed down from a fight. That had endeared him to very few people, particularly since Honor had been the town's reigning princess.

Despite the opposition to their relationship, Honor had always been his biggest cheerleader. She had believed in him until he'd been arrested for burning down the church. Still, after all this time, it gutted him to have caused her such heartache.

Joshua shrugged off the feelings of guilt and recrimination. He had worked steadfastly over the years to redeem his character. He had painstakingly rebuilt his life, laying the foundation one brick at a time. God was a central part of his world now and he lived life with a purpose.

Coming back to his hometown hadn't been easy, but he owed it to his grandfather to pay him his last respects and to tidy up his affairs. He hadn't realized things with the Diamond R would be so complicated.

Joshua made his way to the room he was using as Violet's nursery. Once he entered the bedroom, he stood by her crib and gently rocked her from side to side. When he felt her head droop against his chest, he slowly lowered her until she was resting on her back. Her eyelids were closed and she was peacefully asleep. He quietly made his way back downstairs.

For Violet's sake, he felt grateful that he could finally hold his head up high in Love. He had put the shameful events of his past in the rearview mirror. He felt proud of himself, if only because he knew so many people had given up on him. This town had viewed him as irredeemable and broken. They had been dead wrong.

Joshua hadn't expected to feel such a wealth of emotions upon his return to Love. As soon as he had spotted Kachemak Bay from his seat in the seaplane, he'd felt a tightening sensation in his chest. Despite everything, this town still lived and breathed in him, just like Honor Prescott. One look in her blue-gray eyes had shown him that the past was still a powerful force to be reckoned with.

As Joshua walked back toward the homestead and away from her with his baby girl, Honor's shoulders sagged. Her cheeks felt flushed. Joshua had a child!

She'd been composed during their encounter, even though seeing Joshua holding his daughter had shaken her to the core. Her limbs were trembling. Coming face-to-face with her ex-fiancé hadn't been on her agenda for today. And it had been shocking to realize he was a father. She felt as if someone had just thrown an ice-cold bucket of water over her head. Joshua looked even more handsome than she remembered. Age had only enhanced his masculine appeal. At six feet or so, Joshua's frame had filled out, giving him a more rugged appearance. His dark hair set off against his blue eyes made a striking combination. He was the type of man who drew stares when he walked down the street.

Her mind veered toward Violet. It had hurt her to see the child nestled in Joshua's arms. It served as a stark reminder of the child she had miscarried six years ago. Joshua's child. She pushed the painful feelings away. She couldn't allow herself to get consumed by the past. It might drag her under.

As she exited the stable, Honor spotted Lee, who was quickly making his way toward her. With his salt-and-pepper-colored hair and sea green eyes, Lee had a distinguished appearance. There was something so solid about him. He was trusted by the whole town. At the moment he had an intense expression etched on his face. His movements seemed full of urgency.

"Honor, it's nice to see you," Lee said, warmth emanating from his voice.

"Hey, Lee," Honor said. "Good morning."

Lee ran his hand around his shirt collar. His fingers seemed unsteady. "Under the circumstances, I'm sorry to have called you out here. It was a mistake."

She frowned at him. He looked flustered. Normally, he was a calm, unflappable man. It was slightly alarming to see him acting this way.

Was Lee referencing Joshua's unexpected appearance at the ranch? Like most of the townsfolk, he was fully aware of their history.

"There's been a bit of a hiccup regarding the reading of the will and Bud's property," he said, his tone apologetic. His eyes radiated disappointment. "I probably jumped the gun by inviting you here to the Diamond R."

"What's wrong?" she asked. Adrenaline began to race through her veins. Instinctively, she steeled herself for bad news.

Lee let out a ragged sigh. "Bud didn't update his will, Honor. He made no written provisions to donate the property to the land preservation society." Lee threw his hands in the air. "There's not a whole lot more I can say, but I'm very disappointed."

"What?" Honor exploded. "That can't be right. He said it over and over again. Everyone in town knew his wishes."

Lee shook his head. "According to his attorney, Bud had the best of intentions, but he passed away before he could make it official. He never updated his will. Knowing Bud, he probably figured he had plenty of years ahead to make those changes."

Honor felt numb as the ramifications of Lee's disclosure began to settle in. "He verbally stated his intentions on several occasions. We all knew what he wanted to do with regard to the ranch. Isn't that enough?"

Lee stared at her with sadness radiating from his eyes. "I'm afraid not, Honor. Our hands are pretty much tied. We could file suit against the estate, but it would cost a fortune. And to what avail? Alaskan inheritance law is very clear."

Her heart sank. "So what happens now?" she asked. "Who inherits the property?"

"According to Bud's attorney, Theo and Joshua and another relative named Violet are listed as the heirs to the Diamond R and all of its assets and acreage."

Honor let out a deep breath. She felt like a deflated balloon. The old adage was true: don't count your chickens until they're hatched. In her mind she'd formulated so many plans for the expansion of the wildlife center. Now, in a puff of smoke, those dreams had been dashed.

Lee stroked his chin. "I've heard some rumblings about a developer from Texas who's been circling around trying to buy up property in Love. It seems that Theo has already been in contact with them. They came to the ranch first thing this morning." His chest heaved as he sighed. "There's no easy way to say this, Honor, but I think we have to prepare ourselves for what lies ahead."

Anger flared through her at the idea of Theo making deals to desecrate Bud's ranch. Even as a kid he had never had an appreciation for the ranch. Joshua had been the one who had loved horses, the cowboy lifestyle and riding across the property with Bud. Honor had always thought of Joshua as her hometown cowboy.

"Lee, give it to me straight," Honor demanded. Having grown up with three older brothers, she knew when she was being treated with kid gloves. She had always fought against it. She was way tougher than she might look on the surface.

"Do you remember the town council meeting where

we discussed the upsurge in interest from developers in acquiring land here in Love?" Lee asked.

"Yes," she said with a nod. "With the popularity of Operation Love, this town has been in the media spotlight. And now that Lovely Boots has taken off, a lot of developers view this town as a hot commodity."

Operation Love was a matchmaking program created by Honor's grandfather, Jasper Prescott. As town mayor, Jasper had devised a way of fixing the imbalance in the male-female ratio in town by bringing eligible women to town who were seeking Alaskan bachelors. The program had been very successful, with dozens of marriages and engagements. And Jasper's wife, Hazel Tookes Prescott, had created genuine Alaskan boots that the town had mass produced as a way of boosting the local economy. After years of recession, it had been a brilliant way of bringing revenue to a cash-strapped town.

The downside of her grandfather's matchmaking program and Hazel's creativity was the sudden focus on their Alaskan hamlet. Suddenly, developers were viewing Love as a potential moneymaker. The idea of developers swooping down and buying up Alaskan land only to dig it up and build businesses on it made her sick to her stomach.

Lee's features creased with tension. "This one outfit is serious about buying land here in Love and the Diamond R property is on their radar." His mouth tightened. "It seems they have plans to build a five-star Alaskan dude ranch. There's a chain of them all across the country."

Honor's jaw dropped. A dude ranch! Right here in Love?

"Theo and Joshua probably had a big check waved in front of their eyes by these developers." He made a tutting sound. "They might find it hard to turn down such a lucrative offer."

She let out a shocked sound. Joshua was in on it? She was stunned that he would go along with such a materialistic scheme. Was this the real reason the brothers had made their way back to their hometown? To make a quick buck by selling the Diamond R Ranch and the surrounding property?

"He wouldn't," she murmured. "He's always loved this ranch."

Lee narrowed his gaze as he looked at her. "Never say never, Honor. It's been quite some time since you've known what Joshua may or may not do."

"Is there any way to intervene?" she asked, instantly discouraged by the defeated expression stamped on Lee's face.

"There's nothing more for us to do except say a few prayers," Lee said with a shrug. "Maybe the Ransom heirs will do the right thing and fulfill Bud's heartfelt wishes." He shook his head. "It's doubtful though. Theo seemed very cocky about being owner of the ranch. Something tells me he won't budge an inch."

Anger rose up inside her. She felt her cheeks getting heated. How could they even consider such a drastic move? It went against everything Bud had stood for in this world. It would be fine by Honor if the property wasn't handed over to the town, just so long as it wasn't torn up to create a tacky dude ranch. She didn't want the town of Love to become a commercial enterprise. Her hometown was a small fishing village filled with God-fearing people who loved the quaint and charming aspects of their town. If the Ransom brothers decided to sell, it would be a nightmare for the residents of Love.

Her stomach churned with worry. Hadn't Joshua just told her he would be heading home after settling his grandfather's affairs? Clearly he wasn't invested in the ranch or in this town. Honor fumed. Joshua might not care about the fate of the Diamond R or this town, but she cared deeply about its future.

"There may not be anything we can do to change their minds," she said in a fierce tone. "But I'm going to let Joshua Ransom know exactly what I think of him turning his back on a town he used to call home."

Chapter Two

Joshua threw his hands up in defeat as he gave in to temptation and moved toward the side window so he could check up on Honor. Was she still outside? He pushed back the curtain and peered out the window, keeping his eyes peeled on the stables. Honor was standing with Lee and they seemed to be having a very intense discussion. He watched as she threw her hands in the air and kicked her booted foot in the snow. The gesture almost made him chuckle. Some things never changed. Although most of the townsfolk had always regarded her as sweetness and light, Honor Prescott had always possessed a feisty side. He remembered it well. More times than he'd like to admit, he had been the recipient of her ire. He sighed. Joshua knew he hadn't made it easy for Honor to love him.

But she had loved him, hadn't she? *Love never fails.* How many times had Honor said those words to him, quoting the verse from *Corinthians*? In the end, their love hadn't been strong enough to survive adversity. It had withered and died. And he had walked around with a broken heart for years, pining for the one who'd got-

ten away. That was a long time ago though. He no longer harbored any love for his ex-fiancée. It had taken
years, but he'd finally gotten over her.

He probably shouldn't be spying on Honor, but his
curiosity had gotten the best of him. What was she
doing here in the first place? And what was she discussing with Lee that had become so contentious?

All in all, it had been a strange morning at the ranch.
Theo had met not only with Lee and his grandfather's
attorney, but with a developer from Texas who had
come to discuss the Diamond R Ranch. Joshua hadn't
attended the meeting. His hands had been full with
wrangling a cranky Violet.

Joshua turned away from the window and gazed at
his surroundings. His grandfather was all around him
at the ranch, but especially in this very room. The den
had been Bud's favorite place in the house. Before she
had passed away, his grandmother, Pearl, had always
enjoyed teasing her husband about holing up inside his
man cave for hours on end. Joshua could hear her voice
now. *Bud Ransom, we might as well put a bed and a
stove in there with you. Then you'd never come out.*

He missed both his grandparents. They had been
two of the most loving, generous people he had ever
known. They had doted on him during his childhood
and shown him unconditional love. His own parents
were living in Singapore, too far away to come back
for the memorial service. For all intents and purposes,
his family had been reduced to a small circle.

Did a person ever stop yearning for the ones they
had loved and lost? Honor's face flashed before his
eyes. Beautiful, headstrong Honor. He now knew for
certain he wasn't over the events of the past. Not by a

long shot. Seeing her in the flesh had proven that point. After all this time he still felt a pull in her direction. Not that it mattered. She had shown him years ago that he was dispensable. Honor had tossed him aside like yesterday's garbage. He imagined the whole town of Love had stood up and cheered her on.

A sudden noise drew his attention. Joshua cocked his ear to the side and listened for any cries. These days it seemed as if he was always bracing for the slightest sounds. It was amazing how a child could alter a person's life. He exhaled as silence reigned. Suddenly, Joshua heard the slam of the front door, followed by heavy footsteps. He was about to give Theo a piece of his mind. How many times had he warned him about making loud, disruptive noises when a baby was in the house?

All of a sudden, Honor was standing in the doorway of the den, her hands strategically placed on her hips. Pure molten fire radiated from her eyes. Little huffing sounds were coming from her mouth. He was fairly certain steam was coming out of her ears.

"Are you seriously considering selling out?" she asked in a raised voice, quickly swallowing up the distance between them.

Honor had come charging up to him like a wild bull reacting to a red flag. If she hadn't looked so angry, he might have laughed at her aggressive stance. Her arms were folded across her chest, and she was breathing heavily as she glared at him. She was tapping one of her feet on the hardwood floor.

Old memories crashed over him in unrelenting waves. How could he have forgotten this defiant side of Honor?

He held up his hands. "Can you lower your voice to a dull roar? Slow down. What are you talking about?"

"Lee said there's a developer who wants to buy the Diamond R. He says they want to build a resort on the property—some bootleg version of a dude ranch for people who want a so-called authentic Alaskan cowboy experience."

Joshua stiffened. Hadn't Theo said to keep things quiet about the offer from the developers? Clearly his brother had been running his mouth about the subject. And he had failed to mention anything about a dude ranch. Typical Theo.

He let out a sigh. "Nothing has been decided yet. I just found out about it myself."

Her face fell. "So you're admitting someone is circling around and making an offer on the ranch?"

"Yes, Honor. It's true. Theo told me there's an outfit from Texas that's very interested in buying the property."

"Bud would never have wanted this place to be sold to a developer. How can you even consider it?" she asked, her voice ringing out in the stillness of the room.

Joshua clenched his teeth at the accusatory tone of her voice. He felt his anger rising.

"Excuse me? I don't reckon you want to pick a fight with me over my family's land." He hadn't meant for his voice to have such a hard edge to it, but so be it. He hadn't come back to Love in order to be pushed around and judged by his ex-fiancée. The days of everyone here in town making him feel less than were over. "It's nobody's business but ours."

Honor let out a shocked gasp. She took a few steps closer to him until he could hear her breathing. He could see the flecks in her blue-gray eyes. She was bristling with rage.

"Do you know what will happen to this land if you sell? This developer will come in and tear up the land and make it some ghastly commercial enterprise."

Joshua frowned. "You're getting way ahead of yourself."

"Am I? These things seem to happen fairly quickly. One minute they're making you an offer and the next thing you know papers are being signed. This is precious land. It shouldn't be transformed into something unrecognizable. And Bud wanted to donate the property so it would be preserved from developers."

"Then why didn't he put it in writing and make it official?" Joshua asked. "Bud was smart. He knew the risks in not following through on his promise."

"I—I don't know, but I do believe it was his intention." She locked eyes with him. "Doesn't that mean anything to you?"

"This isn't just up to me. Theo has some say in this as well. And I'm not convinced Bud wanted to donate the property to land preservation. He was as sharp as a tack. Maybe he changed his mind."

He watched as Honor's eyes widened and her mouth opened. Just as she seemed ready to erupt, a loud wail rang out in the room.

Honor froze at the sound. She turned toward the sound of the cries, which came from a nearby baby monitor.

"Is something wrong with Violet?" she asked. She sounded alarmed.

"I'm sure she's fine. She's been fussy since we arrived here," he answered in a clipped tone. "She must have woken up from her nap."

"She sounds upset." Honor bit her lip and looked in the direction of the baby monitor.

"Sometimes she just needs to settle back down."

She swung her gaze back toward him. "Aren't you going to go get her?"

Joshua frowned. He didn't understand why Honor looked so stricken. Was she suggesting he was neglecting Violet? He opened his mouth to say something, but he shut it. He didn't need to remind Honor that she wasn't a parent. There was already enough acrimony between them.

It really didn't matter what she thought. He was Violet's father. He knew what his own daughter needed better than anyone.

"I need to go see to her," Joshua said in an abrupt tone. He turned on his heel and left the room, his footsteps echoing in his wake. Honor turned toward the baby monitor. She could still hear soft cries emanating from it. It caused a tightening sensation in her chest.

Honor hadn't meant to sound so bossy, but the sound of Violet's cries had been tugging at her heartstrings. There was something so poignant about the sound of a baby crying. Tears sprang to her eyes and she blinked them away. She knew it had everything to do with the baby she had lost. Joshua's child. Although her own pregnancy had been unexpected, Honor had desperately wanted to be a mother. Not being able to hold her child in her arms was something she would never get over. And at moments like this one, the pain of loss came crashing over her in waves.

A few minutes later, the sound of footsteps heralded Joshua's return. Honor's gaze went immediately to Violet. The baby's eyes were slightly red-rimmed and her hair was rumpled. She looked adorable.

Honor's pulse began to quicken at the sight of Joshua and his little girl.

Violet was the perfect name for the blue-eyed stunner squirming in Joshua's arms. With her chubby cheeks and a head of blond curls, Violet was a vision. Unable to stop herself, Honor took two steps toward Joshua, then reached out and grasped one of Violet's fingers.

"How old is she?" Honor asked, filled with curiosity.

"She's ten months old."

Her throat felt as dry as sandpaper. There were other questions she wanted to ask, but she wasn't sure it was really her place. Where was Violet's mother? she wondered. She cast another gaze at his ring finger to make sure she hadn't missed it. He definitely wasn't wearing a wedding band.

"Bud said you'd gotten divorced a long time ago," she blurted out, immediately wishing she could pull back the impulsive words. She didn't want Joshua to think she'd been keeping tabs on him. Bud had hired her to come over to the Diamond R twice a week to check in on his animals. Although he'd never divulged much about Joshua's life, he had slipped one day and confided in her about Joshua's divorce.

"That's right," he said, jutting his chin out. "About five years ago. It lasted all of eleven months. I'm no longer married."

Honor knew the shock was showing on her face.

Her entire life people had told her about her inability to hide her feelings. She was certain this moment wasn't any exception. She was reacting to the fact that Joshua hadn't married Violet's mother. It wasn't shocking in itself, but it didn't gel with the Joshua Ransom she had once known.

Joshua Ransom was no longer her business. What difference did it make whether he was single or divorced or had a houseful of babies? It was none of her concern. He was nothing more than a faded memory to her.

"Dada," Violet said in a sing-song voice, looking up at Joshua with a gummy smile.

"Hi there," Honor said in a light voice, smiling at the blue-eyed charmer. "Aren't you the sweetest little thing?"

Violet gifted her with a grin, then reached out and tugged at her hair. Honor let out a squeal as Violet grabbed a few strands and wrapped them around her fingers. The expression on Violet's face was one of triumph.

"Easy there, Vi," Joshua said with a low chuckle. He began disentangling Honor's hair from Violet's grasp. "She loves to latch onto things."

"She's beautiful," Honor said, unable to take her eyes off the little girl. She looked dainty in her pink-and-purple onesie, yet her little body appeared to be sturdy and well nourished. From the looks of it, Joshua was doing a great job in the fatherhood department. There was a funny feeling stirring around in her belly.

"Thank you," Joshua said. "She's changed my life in ways I never could have imagined." Joshua's voice was filled with reverence. "On a cloudy day, this little lady can make the sun peek out past the clouds."

"And her mother? Is she here, too?" she asked, her heart sinking at the idea of coming face-to-face with the woman who had given Joshua a child. It was a petty emotion, but Honor couldn't ignore it. It was an unsettling feeling. After six long years she shouldn't care about Joshua's personal life.

Joshua's expression hardened. His jaw tightened. "She passed away right after Violet was born. I'm raising her on my own."

Guilt clawed at her. Moments ago she'd felt an emotion resembling jealousy. And now she had just discovered that Violet didn't have a mother. The situation was heartbreaking. Joshua was a single father raising a baby daughter. And poor Violet would never know the woman who had given her life.

It was incredibly difficult to reconcile the man standing in front of her cradling Violet with the ex-fiancé who had run wild all over town, leaving mayhem in his wake. He had once stolen a car as a prank and broken into a Jarvis Street shop named Keepsakes on a dare. And in one final act of rebellion, he had gone too far and started a fire that had destroyed the town's beloved church. A local man had sustained burns after trying to put out the blaze. There had been no going back for Joshua after that heinous act. It had earned him a one-way ticket out of Love.

She shook the painful memories off and focused on the present. "I'm sorry to hear that, Joshua. It's terribly sad for both of you," she said in a low voice.

"Yes. It's not fair for Violet. She'll never get to know her mother," Joshua said. He sighed deeply. "Tomorrow is never promised, like Bud always said. Life keeps teaching me that lesson. I thought I'd be able to see my grandfather again. He had plans to fly to Seattle to visit Violet and me next month." His mouth quirked. "That won't happen now."

There was nothing Honor could say. No words were necessary. They both knew from their own experiences how unfair life could be. At the age of eight, Joshua had lost a baby sister to leukemia while Honor had struggled throughout her life with having parents who were missing in action. But developing a relationship with God during her college years had strengthened her as a person. He had shown her that despite setbacks and disappointments, life was a beautiful journey.

Honor found her gaze straying back toward Violet time and again. She felt a wild impulse to ask Joshua if she could hold his daughter. She wanted to cradle her tightly in her arms and smell her forehead. Babies always smelled like powder and soap and fresh flowers. She knew it wasn't true, but looking at Violet made her believe it.

Seeing Joshua's child created an ache deep within her soul.

"I need to get back to the wildlife center," Honor said, tearing her gaze away from Violet. She needed to get away from Violet and Joshua as quickly as possible. These tender feelings were making her feel all jumbled up inside. A feeling of intense loss swept over her. Thinking about the baby she'd lost was incredibly painful. Joshua's child. Seeing Violet brought back those devastating memories. What she wouldn't have given to have held her own child in her arms just once.

She had only come to the Diamond R Ranch today

to meet with Lee about Bud's will. Seeing Joshua had been a complete shock to the system. And finding out that Joshua had a sweet-faced baby girl had been quite the surprise. Her mind was still whirling about the terms of Bud's will. It was all a little much for her to absorb at the moment.

Honor had no intention of allowing herself to get swept up in Joshua's life. When she had ended their engagement, Honor had cut all ties with him. Joshua had torn her world apart and ripped her heart to shreds. Becoming invested in his life was a surefire way to blur the lines she had established between them. She couldn't run the risk of falling for him all over again. The sight of him holding Violet threatened to wear down all her defenses. It made her wonder what kind of a father he would have been to their child.

Joshua eyed her warily. "Are you finished reading me the riot act?"

She locked gazes with him. "For now," she said in a low voice. "I don't want to startle Violet by raising my voice." On impulse, she reached out and swept a finger across the baby's cheek. She was soft and warm. *She is more precious than rubies.* Honor felt a tugging sensation in the region of her heart as she gazed upon the irresistible sight of Joshua's baby girl.

"By the way, no decision has been made regarding the Diamond R," Joshua said in a firm voice. "But make no mistake, Honor. Any decision I make will be in the best interest of Violet and her future. The moment I became her father she became my number one priority in this world. Bar none."

She nodded in his direction as an acknowledgment of the sentiments he had just expressed. Putting his daughter first was noble. She had no idea what that meant for the future of the ranch. If she believed Joshua, its destiny still hung in the balance.

As Honor walked away from Joshua and Violet and out into the brisk February afternoon, a feeling of sadness swept over her. Six years ago she would have given anything to have this version of Joshua Ransom in her life. Steady. Devoted. Strong. Dependable. Instead, she had fallen for a rebellious rabble-rouser who had stolen her heart, then made a fool of her in front of her family and the whole town. Ever since then Honor had been wary of falling in love.

Tears pooled in her eyes as the dreams of her youth came rising back to the surface with a vengeance. She had once dreamed of forever with Joshua. She'd wanted the fairy tale—the white picket fence, the blue-eyed babies who were the spitting image of their father and a happily-ever-after. None of it had come true.

Her brothers had all found their happily-ever-afters. Boone had married the love of his life, Grace, and they now had a baby girl named Eva. Cameron had reunited with Paige and discovered he was a father to baby Emma. Liam had been given the greatest gift of all when he'd discovered that his wife, Ruby, who had been presumed dead in an avalanche, was alive and suffering from amnesia. Their reunion had been incredibly moving. Even Jasper had found everlasting love with Hazel. The list went on and on. Declan. Finn. Sophie. It was as if the whole world was coupling up and finding their happy endings. Everyone but her.

All this time Honor had been telling herself she didn't want love in her life. But it had been a big lie. Being wounded by her failed relationship with Joshua had made her gun-shy. She wanted the same things her siblings had—promises of forever. But having all her dreams go up in flames six years ago had left her with permanent scars. Even though she had a good idea of the life she wanted to live, she had no idea how to reach out and grab it.

Once Honor left the ranch, Joshua brought Violet into the kitchen so he could whip up some lunch for her. Introducing Violet to his ex-fiancée had been a bit surreal. Two worlds colliding. He hadn't bothered to tell Honor that Violet wasn't his biological child. Truthfully, it wasn't anyone's business. In his heart, she was every bit his daughter. When his ex-wife, Lauren, had discovered she had a terminal illness, she had tracked him down and begged him to raise Violet. Although he hadn't seen Lauren in over two years, Joshua had embraced her request. It had been the single best decision he'd ever made in his life.

Joshua let out a low chuckle as he placed his daughter in the wooden high chair he had retrieved from the attic. It looked like something from the Stone Age. He imagined his grandparents had used it for his own father and perhaps him and Theo as well. He had been surprised at its sturdiness. Built to last. He had always thought of the Diamond R Ranch in the same vein. Enduring.

Joshua placed Violet in the high chair, then bent over so he could place a kiss on her temple. "This thing might be old, but it does the job, doesn't it, cutie pie?" Violet looked at him and gurgled. He took that as a yes.

Footsteps announced Theo's arrival in the kitchen. His brother stood in the entryway with a huge grin on his face. With his dark head of hair and azure-colored eyes, Theo could easily pass for his twin. Growing up, they had constantly been confused for one another by teachers and townsfolk.

"Be careful, bro. You're turning into a pile of mush," Theo teased. "That little charmer has you wrapped around her finger."

Joshua felt a slight twinge of embarrassment. He had always prided himself on being rugged and manly. That's the way he and Theo had been raised. Now Theo had caught him in the act of cooing to his baby girl and mashing up peas and carrots and pastini for her lunch.

Why should he worry about what he looked like? He loved his daughter more than anything in this world. He had always cared way too much about his older brother's opinion. Doing so hadn't always been in Joshua's best interest. It had ended up costing him a lot.

"Fatherhood changes a man," he conceded, not even bothering to object to Theo's observation. If being mushy brought him one step closer to being a phenomenal father, Joshua would assume the title as the mushiest guy in all of Alaska.

Theo took off his cowboy hat and rocked back on his heels. "Was that Honor Prescott I just saw beating a fast path away from here on a horse? She was riding like the wind itself was chasing her."

Joshua didn't really want to discuss Honor with his brother, but there was no way of avoiding it. Theo had made it clear on numerous occasions how he felt about his ex-fiancée. *Stuck-up* and *highfalutin* were two words he had regularly used to describe her. It had annoyed Joshua to no end. Theo hadn't known Honor. Not the way Joshua had. She had been sweet and loyal and kind. The best person he'd ever known. And if he hadn't messed things up so royally, she would have become his wife.

"Yes, it was Honor," he admitted. "She came here to meet up with Lee. And then she blasted me regarding your meeting with the developers. She was really bent out of shape at the idea of us selling the Diamond R." He hated the way Honor had made him feel. The way she had spoken to him had been harsh, as if he was a traitor to his grandfather and the entire town. Even though a part of him rejected her assessment of the situation, he still felt a bit tarnished by her judgment. Old habits died hard. Sadly, it was a familiar feeling in this town.

Theo's expression hardened. "Same small-minded opinions," he scoffed. "Some things never change. These people seem to think they have some say in the matter, when in reality it's Ransom family business."

"Please don't tell me they're really intending to open an Alaskan dude ranch," Joshua said. "That's about the cheesiest thing I've ever heard."

"They mentioned it in passing," Theo said with a shrug. "But, to be honest, it's not my concern. What they do with the property is their business."

Joshua frowned at his brother. "Sounds like you've already made up your mind. We've barely discussed it."

Theo scoffed. "Is there really anything to think about? Let's face it, Joshua. Neither one of us wants to live in this Podunk town. It would be about as exciting as watching paint dry to stay here. I for one could use a big fat check from this Texas corporation. They sound as if they're ready to make a very lucrative offer and draw up contracts."

Joshua's head felt as if it was spinning. He'd barely been back in Love for twenty-four hours and not only had he inherited the Diamond R Ranch, but he might end up a millionaire if he agreed to sell the property. That type of money would be instrumental in raising Violet and paying for her future education.

Coming face-to-face with Honor had knocked him off balance. She represented all of his young hopes and dreams. There had never been another great love in his life after Honor Prescott. She had imprinted herself on his heart. And even though he shouldn't care about her opinion, he still did. He wanted her to see the new and improved Joshua. It had hurt him to see such condemnation flashing in her eyes.

Everything was happening way too fast for his liking. The idea of selling his family's ranch felt incredibly final. And if Honor was right, it wasn't in accordance with his grandfather's wishes. But Theo wanted to make the deal, collect the money and then head out of Dodge. It was a lot to process.

"Theo, I need some time to wrap my head around all of this. Why don't we focus on the memorial service? After all, it's the main reason we came here, isn't it? To honor Gramps."

Theo nodded. "You're right. Let's give him a fitting send-off." He rubbed his hands together. "How about a rip-roaring barbecue at the ranch?"

"It's February in Alaska. It's far from barbecue weather." Joshua chuckled. "How about a simple church service followed by a nice meal and fellowship with some of his friends?" Joshua suggested.

"A church service?" Theo asked with wide eyes. "Not sure we'd be welcome in church, Joshua. Not after what happened with the fire."

"Our grandfather paid our debts at that church. He donated a hefty sum of money to have it rebuilt. I managed to dodge jail time due to my age, but I still had to attend a program for first-time offenders before I went overseas." Joshua winced. He hated discussing that period of his life. It hadn't been pretty. "Pastor Jack reached out to me and extended an olive branch. He wants us to host the memorial for Bud there. He was beloved in this town. Thankfully, the townsfolk could separate Gramps from the actions of his grandsons." He shook his head, overwhelmed by the pastor's generosity. Not many people would be gracious toward the man who they believed was responsible for burning down the town's church.

"Joshua," Theo said in a low voice. "Maybe it's time for me to set the record straight. It's not fair you've been blamed all this time for something I did."

He waved a hand at his brother. "It's water under the bridge. We made the decision to protect your army career. If I hadn't claimed responsibility, you would have lost your military position."

Theo made a strangled sound. "So instead you lost the woman you loved and were run out of town on a rail. It doesn't seem fair, does it?"

Even after all these years it still hurt to think about the dissolution of his relationship with Honor and being disowned by his hometown. At the time, it had felt like the end of the world. It had forever altered the course of his life.

He shrugged. "I wasn't exactly innocent, Theo. I

was right there with you causing trouble. We had no business being in the church at night."

"But I set the fire. You didn't. I was playing around with my lighter and one of the hymnals. When the flame began raging out of control, I had no clue how to put it out. I was frightened."

Joshua nodded. The event was indelibly imprinted on his mind. "So we ran. Probably the worst thing we could have done," Joshua said. "The church might have been salvageable if we'd stuck around and called the authorities." After all this time, he still felt guilty. If only he'd convinced Theo to alert law enforcement. If he was being honest with himself, he knew why he hadn't done so. Sheriff Boone Prescott. He hadn't wanted to give Honor's brother the satisfaction of saying I-told-you-so to his fiancée. They had been caught anyway.

Joshua turned to Violet and spooned a mouthful of food into her mouth. Although he appreciated his brother's desire to make amends, Joshua knew it wouldn't do much good in the present. He had lost Honor because of one foolish decision that had spiraled out of control. The town had been rocked by the torched church and the knowledge that the fire had been started by one of their own.

Joshua raked his hand through his hair. Now he couldn't hold back the groundswell of memories rising up inside him. "Zachariah Cummings spotted us as we fled the scene. He told the authorities I was the one covered in ash and fleeing the church. He mistook you for me. Same hair and eye color. Same build."

"Zachariah tried to put out the fire by himself before the authorities arrived," Theo said, a look of discomfort stamped on his face.

"He suffered serious burns," Joshua said with a shake of his head. "He's lucky to be alive."

Theo groaned. "It was all my fault. And you took the fall because my stint in the army would have been over before it really began."

The brothers locked gazes. So many words had been left unspoken between them. Joshua had taken the blame to protect his brother's military future. As a result, he had lost everything. "But I'm no longer in the army, and you deserve to be vindicated." Theo's voice rang out with conviction.

"Theo, I've moved on since then. It won't serve a single purpose to rehash the past and dig up old wounds. In a few weeks we'll both be back home in Seattle and Los Angeles living our lives. I can't imagine either one of us having a reason to come back here." Just saying the words out loud caused a tightening sensation smack-dab in the center of his chest. It sounded so final.

For a few moments silence settled over the kitchen. Violet's gibberish was the only sound in the room. She was in her own world and babbling away. Joshua imagined that Theo, much like himself, was consumed by the past, their grandfather's passing and being back in their hometown. Not to mention the dilemma of whether or not to sell the Diamond R.

"We'll have to contact Pastor Jack and get a list together of all his friends here in town," Theo said, breaking the silence.

An invite list. He couldn't help but think about Honor and her big, bustling family. They had always respected and admired his grandfather, but because of the bad feelings between himself and the Prescotts, Joshua wasn't certain if they would attend the memorial service. It made his heart ache a little to think about it. Joshua hoped he hadn't burned all of his bridges in his hometown.

For some reason, being a father had changed his views about Love. It hadn't all been negative. He wanted Violet to know the place where he'd been born and raised. The Diamond R Ranch had been a huge part of his upbringing. He couldn't change the way people felt about his past, but he wanted to show everyone that he had grown and matured.

Even though he had tried to convince himself that he was over the past, it still sat like an anchor on his chest. When he least expected it, memories rose up and threatened to drag him under. Pain. Loss. Heartache. One fateful decision that had altered the course of his young life. He had kicked himself a thousand times for not telling Honor the truth.

Even if he was only in Love for a short duration, Joshua intended to extinguish those painful memories before he headed back to Seattle. Since he'd left town he had worked tirelessly to make something of himself. He now owned a home construction business and he'd been flipping houses to bring in more income. He had stashed away a nice sum of money. In the next few months he intended to purchase a medium-sized starter home for himself and Violet. All in all, life was good.

His life had moved on in the aftermath of the dissolution of his relationship with Honor. When she had broken off their engagement, the very foundation of Joshua's world crumbled. Although he had been forced to adjust to living without her, it had been the most difficult undertaking of his life.

She's too good for you, Ransom.

Those words had been seared into his brain, courtesy of Sheriff Boone Prescott and his brothers. As much as he had hated Boone for being so blunt, Joshua had always known it had been true. Despite having loved her, Joshua knew he hadn't been worthy of the reigning princess of Love, Alaska. Honor had been the shiny brass ring completely out of his reach. Against all odds, he had earned her love, which had made him the happiest man in all of Alaska. But love hadn't been enough.

Joshua winced as bitter memories washed over him. In one reckless moment, Joshua had shown his complete unworthiness and given Honor no choice but to walk away from him. And even though he had moved on, Joshua still wasn't over it. Not by a long shot.

Chapter Three

Honor drove her truck down the snowy streets of downtown Love and hummed to the upbeat tune on the radio. It felt nice to be out and about on a chilly Saturday afternoon. Having brunch with her family provided a well-needed pick-me-up. She had become so isolated working and living out at the wildlife center. As much as she loved her job, it was important to stop every now and again to smell the forget-me-nots.

Her family had been advising her to get out more and start socializing with the townsfolk. Honor knew exactly what it meant. Everyone wanted her to find a nice Alaskan man to settle down and start a family with. It was easier said than done. So far she hadn't been able to let go of the past in order to embrace her future. Her heart had been encased in ice for quite some time. And whenever she thought about opening up to someone, fear of the past repeating itself kept her in the safe zone. It was far better to be single than to be brokenhearted.

As soon as she crossed the threshold of the Moose Café, the tempting smells of freshly brewed coffee and baked bread rose to her nostrils. There was already a bustling crowd scattered about the establishment. Her brother Cameron's café was a very successful eatery here in town. Everyone loved the coffee, the food and the relaxed atmosphere. Honor was proud of her older brother for living out his dreams and pushing past all the self-doubt.

"Honor! It's nice to see you." Sophie Catalano, Honor's dear friend and a waitress-barista at the Moose Café, warmly greeted her. "You barely show your face around here anymore."

"Hey, Sophie," Honor said, wrapping her arms around the beautiful redhead for a warm hug. "It's great to see you. I've been so busy at the wildlife center it's hard to get to town most days."

"I understand," Sophie said with a smile. "You're doing important work over there. Ruby was raving about your workshop on birds of prey. Aidan was mighty impressed," she said, referring to Honor's seven-year-old nephew.

"Wait till he finds out we have some lynx kittens that were orphaned and injured in a fire. He's such a compassionate little boy. I know he'll want to come see them as soon as he can get over there." Just the thought of the lynx kittens made Honor smile. It had been so fortunate that a local firefighter, Hank Jeffries, had managed to rescue them from the fire. They were now out of danger and on their way to a full recovery.

"You're pretty much the bee's knees as far as Aidan is concerned," Sophie said.

Honor grinned so wide her cheeks hurt with the effort. "I think that's probably the best compliment I've ever received." Just the thought of her nephew and nieces filled Honor with joy. Her brothers had made her such a proud auntie. Family meant the world to her and God had blessed her with all of these connections.

"If you're looking for your brothers, they're sitting over there with Jasper," Sophie said, nodding in the direction of a table in the back. Honor followed Sophie's gaze, smiling at the sight of all three of her brothers sitting with her grandfather, along with Declan and Finn O'Rourke, close friends of all the Prescotts. None of her sisters-in-law were present, which made Honor the only female in attendance. She looked around for Hazel. It always felt nice to have some extra estrogen when surrounded by Prescott and O'Rourke men.

Honor walked over to the table and quietly joined her family. She was greeted by a chorus of enthusiastic voices. Warmth settled in her chest. This was home, she thought. A place where you were greeted with joy and open arms. Unconditional love. She settled into a seat beside Boone and Liam. It felt nice to be surrounded by family and good friends. She felt safe and protected from the slings and arrows of life. Honor might disagree with them from time to time, but when times were tough, they all had each other's backs.

Hazel—Jasper's wife and a surrogate mother to Honor and her siblings—strolled over to the table clutching papers against her chest. She looked around the table and flashed a wide smile. "Morning everyone. Glad you could all make it. Isn't it nice to get together and break bread? I can't wait for you to taste my new jalapeño corn fritters."

Jasper looked at Hazel. "You know I don't like spicy food. It gives me heartburn. Can you please just cut to the chase and tell us why you organized this brunch?

You're about as transparent as glass. It's obvious you have something up your sleeve."

Hazel slapped Jasper on the shoulder, causing him to let out a yelp. "Old Jasper here is right. I've made up some flyers and I'm going to be distributing them to our customers today. Then I'm going to hang some up at the church on the announcement board."

"If this is about your over-the-top birthday party," Jasper groused, "we already know you've planned your own shindig. Everyone has already saved the date and placed it on their calendars."

"Once again, you're wrong, Jasper." Hazel swung her gaze around the table. "To be frank, I really don't want to hear any grumbling about this. I just wanted to give you all a heads-up." She placed the papers down on the table with a thump, then eyeballed everyone as if daring them to say something.

Honor picked up one of the flyers. It had the café's logo at the top. She read the words out loud. "Home-going reception in honor of Bud Ransom."

Liam sputtered as he drank his coffee. "Here? At the Moose Café?" he asked, his eyes bulging.

Cameron held up his hands. "Don't blame me. I had nothing to do with it. I just own the joint," he muttered.

"Was this all your idea, Hazel?" Honor asked with a frown. Never in a million years would she have imagined that the Ransom brothers would be welcome at the Moose Café. It felt like something in the universe had shifted.

Hazel grinned. "Yep. It was all me. I figured after the memorial service we could all come here for some refreshments and fellowship. Joshua and Theo were at the church looking for a place to hold a reception, so I suggested they have it here."

"What in the world did you do that for?" Jasper asked. "Those Ransom boys are nothing but trouble. Always have been. Always will be. And I can't believe either one of 'em had the nerve to step inside a church."

Honor cringed at the harsh tone of her grandfather's voice. By force of habit she opened her mouth to stick up for Joshua, then quickly shut it. It wasn't her job to take up for Joshua anymore. Those days were long over.

"To be fair," Liam said, "that was a long time ago. None of us would want to be judged by our worst moment."

Honor ached at the sincerity in her brother's voice. Of all her siblings, Liam was the one who was the most forgiving. As a physician, he didn't have the luxury to judge others. All who sought medical help from him were treated with equal kindness and dedication.

"Bud was a fine man, but that's where it ends as far as his family is concerned," Boone said, folding his arms across his chest. "Theo and Joshua haven't been part of the fabric of this town for quite some time. They burned those bridges a long time ago, no pun intended. I'm surprised they'd want to host something here."

Declan flashed a pearly grin. "It might be fun to toss them out on their ears for old time's sake," he said with a laugh.

"You should be ashamed of yourselves!" Hazel barked. "Not an ounce of charity to spare, is that it? Those boys just suffered a great loss. Haven't you ever heard that once you're a part of this town you're always welcomed home with open arms? It's practically the town motto."

"Nope," Cameron said with a shake of his head. "Can't say I have." He squinted at Hazel. "Are you sure you didn't just make that up on the spot?"

Hazel glared at him. "I'm not even going to dignify that with an answer. We're going to let those boys host the reception right here at the Moose."

"They're not exactly boys anymore," Finn said with a snort.

"Troublemakers is what they are," Jasper roared. "I can't think of a single good thing either of those two ever contributed to this town. They weren't happy unless they were causing mayhem and madness." He shook his fist in the air. "You mark my words! If they stick around Love, they'll be up to no good in no time." He swung his gaze toward Honor. "You should thank the Lord Almighty that you didn't marry that scoundrel."

Honor gulped. She didn't even want to think about how angry her family would be when they found out Joshua and Theo were courting an offer from a developer to purchase the Diamond R Ranch. She feared Jasper just might have a coronary. He'd already had one heart attack a few years ago. For the moment she was keeping quiet about it. After all, nothing had been decided. And she really didn't want to raise Jasper's blood pressure. The news would surely put everyone on edge.

Hazel planted her hands on her hips. "The last time I checked, I have some say around here. Long story short, I've invited the Ransom brothers to have a reception here after the memorial service. I don't want to hear another word about it."

Everything stilled and hushed for a moment as the news settled in. Even Jasper kept quiet. There was a don't-mess-with-me vibe radiating from Hazel. No one wanted to see her erupt.

"Well, we might as well order some food," Boone mumbled. "I came over here expecting to be fed. And I know better than to fight with you, Hazel."

"I sure wish Jasper would get that memo," Hazel said, letting out a delighted cackle. "I keep telling him he needs to be sweeter to me since my birthday is coming up. He might not make it onto the invite list."

Jasper grumbled and buried his head in the menu, refusing to meet his wife's gaze. Honor knew her grandfather's anger was genuine. He really disliked both Ransom brothers. Honor knew part of the reason was tied up in her history with Joshua, while another reason lay in Jasper's title as town mayor. It was impossible for her grandfather to respect people who he felt weren't law-abiding citizens. Being responsible for the destruction of the town's church had been unforgiveable in Jasper's eyes. Not to mention the fact that Jasper's close friend Zachariah had been hurt in the fire.

Honor let out a sigh. Jasper wasn't the only one. The majority of the townsfolk in Love had vowed to run Joshua out of town on a rail. It hadn't come to that since Joshua had packed up his things and left Love after she'd broken things off with him.

Brunch was a solemn affair. Everyone dug in to their food and tried to focus on anything but the elephant in the room. At the end of the meal, everyone got up and dispersed without lingering for conversation or fellowship. A disgruntled vibe hung in the air. It made Honor feel uncomfortable. She didn't like her family to be at odds. For a long time after her breakup with Joshua, Honor had been angry at Boone. She had irrationally blamed him for her broken engagement and all the troubles with Joshua. It had taken quite a while for Honor to forgive her brother for opposing their relationship.

As she stood up to leave, Liam placed his arm around her and pulled her off to the side. "How do you feel about all of this? It must be strange to have Joshua back in Love after all this time."

"It's fine," she murmured, meeting Liam's skeptical gaze. She shrugged. "I'll admit it is kind of odd. Seeing him for the first time was surreal. And finding out he has a baby kind of threw me for a loop."

"A baby?" Liam asked. "I heard he had one of those quickie marriages a few years back, but if I recall correctly, they split up shortly after the wedding."

Honor wrinkled her nose. "You're right. He isn't married any longer. And he's raising baby Violet on his own because her mother died."

Liam winced. "That's tough. I know what it's like to raise a child by myself. When Ruby was presumed dead, I was both father and mother to Aidan." He scratched his jaw. "It wasn't easy."

"No," Honor said, squeezing her brother's arm. "I know you went through some hard times. Despite what went down between myself and Joshua, I don't want him to suffer the same way you did."

Liam narrowed his gaze as he looked at her. "Honor, I hope you maintain a safe distance from Joshua."

"What do you mean?" she asked.

"You have a heart that's as wide open as the Alaskan tundra. I don't want you to get hurt again." Liam didn't need to say anything else. It was written all over his handsome face. Her brothers had always been her protectors. Years ago they had tried in vain to get between her and Joshua. Like most young women who were head over heels in love, Honor had been stubborn and intractable. She had felt such resentment toward her brothers for trying to sabotage her youthful romance. There had been no convincing her of the unsuitability of Joshua Ransom.

She had been blind to Joshua's flaws until everything exploded in her face.

"He's only come back for the memorial," she said in a clipped tone. "And, believe it or not, I've moved past my relationship with Joshua." She let out a brittle-sounding laugh. "We were kids back then."

Liam nodded. "Kids who were crazy in love," he noted.

Crazy in love. It was an apt description for the way she had felt about Joshua. And the way he had felt about her in return. They had been madly, deeply, happily in love.

All of sudden Hazel appeared at their side, allowing Honor a reprieve from having to come up with a response to Liam's statement. There was no doubt about it. She and Joshua had been so committed to one another that they had dreamed of getting married and spending their lives together. He had proposed to Honor and put a ring on her finger. Their relationship had been so much more intense than youthful infatuation. Even though she had tried to minimize those feelings over the years in order to make herself feel better about the way things had crashed and burned, it had been the real deal.

Hazel cleared her throat. "Liam. Do you mind if I have a word with Honor?"

"Of course not," Liam said. He winked at Hazel. "She's all yours."

Once they were alone, Hazel began shifting from one foot to the other. A sheepish expression crept over her face.

"Honor, I think I might owe you an apology. Jasper, bless his heart, isn't always on target, but he pointed out that I was wrong to offer the Moose Café to Joshua without checking with you first." She bit her lip. "I know how hard it was when things ended between you and Joshua. Never in a million years would I ever want to cause you any pain."

"Please don't worry about me. I'm fine. I think it was very generous of you to offer the Moose Café to Joshua and Theo."

She groaned. "You're just being nice. I'm sorry if I made a mess of things. Sometimes I try too hard to do what I think is right," she muttered. "Maybe I should have just left things alone."

Honor reached out and took her hand. "Hazel. You didn't do anything wrong. Joshua and I are six years older and wiser. We've both moved on with our lives. What kind of woman would I be if I begrudged them the use of the café for Bud's reception?" No matter what had transpired between her and Joshua in the past, Honor couldn't allow it to change who she was as a person. She had cared for Joshua's grandfather. Bud had been her friend.

"That's very mature of you. Can you do me a favor

and ask your brothers to kick their vendetta to the curb?" She made a tutting sound. "They need to just let it go already. Joshua was a boy of eighteen when he started that fire. It was a terrible accident and he paid dearly for it."

"Yes, he did," Honor murmured, knowing Hazel was referencing her.

"Call me a softie, but life is too short to harbor bitterness in one's heart."

"Old grudges are silly. I don't want anyone feuding on my account. The way I figure it, if I can be civil to Joshua, no one else has the right to act up." She chewed on her lip. "And I hate to say it, but there could be a legitimate reason for tensions to heighten in the near future."

Hazel frowned. "Do I dare ask what you're talking about?"

Honor bit her lip. "I don't want to gossip, but you'll find out soon enough. Bud didn't sign the ranch over to the town and the preservation society. Joshua and Theo are his heirs. And they're considering selling the Diamond R to a Texas developer."

Hazel's eyes bulged. "No! That can't be right!"

"Unfortunately it is. I heard it straight from Lee's mouth and then Joshua confirmed it." She made a face. "Some outfit from Texas wants to create a posh dude ranch on the property. It seems as if everyone wants a piece of our little fishing village these days."

"I'm afraid for this town if they sell out. Bud was a smart man. I can't believe he didn't make things official in his will," Hazel lamented.

Honor shrugged. "I don't know. Maybe he changed his mind about it. Perhaps he wanted Joshua and his daughter to be comfortable. He's raising her all by himself."

"Joshua has a daughter?" Hazel asked. "Years ago I wouldn't have trusted that boy with a pet rock, but time changes folks. Everyone deserves a shot at getting things right."

"I think so, too," Honor concurred. *Getting things right.* Suddenly, a lightbulb went off in Honor's head. "Maybe Joshua will decide to do the right thing regarding the Diamond R. Perhaps this is his chance to redeem himself," she said.

Hazel eyed her with skepticism. "I wouldn't hold my breath. Joshua and Theo are just passing through Love. Neither one of 'em has any reason to hold on to the ranch. Sad to say, but selling it makes a whole lot of sense." Hazel patted her on the shoulder before walking back toward the kitchen.

Honor shook her head. It wasn't going to happen. Not on her watch! There was no way she was going to sit around on the sidelines as a developer destroyed Bud's ranch and created such a monstrosity in Love. She wasn't certain how she would go about it, but she was determined to make Joshua see how wrong it would be to sell the Diamond R Ranch. Perhaps she could remind him of all the reasons he used to adore his hometown and Bud's ranch.

If there was even a sliver of the old Joshua that still existed, Honor felt certain he would tell the Texas developers to take a hike and find a new town to plunder.

Chapter Four

Joshua looked around the Moose Café with keen interest. The establishment owned by Cameron Prescott had a rustic charm. Copper lights hung from the ceiling, giving the café a warm glow. Forget-me-nots had been placed in small vases on each individual table. He had to admit, the place had a comfortable, cozy vibe. The smell of coffee and baked goods went straight to his empty stomach. It grumbled loudly in appreciation. He could see why this place was successful. It was the perfect spot to sit and eat and enjoy fellowship with good friends.

Not that he would ever hang out here. Too many Prescotts and O'Rourkes lurking around. He imagined they wouldn't welcome him with open arms anytime soon if he happened to stroll in on his own. Clearly Hazel had pulled some strings in order to allow them to host the reception here. At first he had balked at the idea, but in reality, there were few places here in town that would host them.

This wasn't about him or the way the townsfolk felt about him. It was about Bud and giving him a proper send-off. Pastor Jack had given a beautiful eulogy for his grandfather. It had been a nice mix of humor, solemnity and faith. Joshua had been incredibly moved and grateful for the kind words.

The café was packed with townsfolk. Everyone had migrated over after the church service. Folks were milling around and gathering in little groups. He ignored the whispers as best he could. After the scandalous way he'd left town, he deserved them. As far as they knew, he was a fire starter.

He swung his gaze around and locked eyes with Boone. The man's expression was shuttered but his eyes glittered with anger. After all these years, the sheriff of Love still couldn't stand the sight of him. It radiated from his every pore. It made sense, Joshua supposed. He watched as a dark-haired woman with striking features gently tugged at Boone's arm, then placed a baby in his arms. His features softened as he looked down at the child and began to nuzzle his nose against hers. Boone appeared to be the epitome of a family man.

So he does have a heart after all, Joshua thought. He wasn't simply a tyrant with a shiny gold badge.

He stuffed down the spark of jealousy at the sight of the family unit. It was what he'd wanted as long as he could remember. A wife and kids. Years ago he had been convinced he and Honor were destined to live out their days together. Sometimes he still allowed himself to daydream about what might have been if he hadn't claimed responsibility for starting the fire.

Joshua cradled Violet closer against his chest and shook off thoughts of the past. He was blessed to have his daughter. Her presence in his life strengthened his sense of purpose. God had answered his prayers in the form of the blue-eyed little girl.

It felt as if he had just walked into the lion's den. Folks were eyeing him warily. Some were glaring at him with outright hostility while others seemed to feel sympathy toward him. Even though Violet was a baby, he prayed she didn't pick up on any negative vibes swirling around the café.

Hazel appeared at his side holding her arms out. "Why don't you let me take Violet and put her down for a nap? That way you can mingle with the guests. Cameron has a playpen in his office he uses for Emma. I'm guessing she'll settle down just fine."

He looked down at Violet. She was nodding off and heading for sleepy-time. It was way past her nap hour. Joshua handed her over to Hazel, who seemed delighted to be holding a baby in her arms. She began to softly hum as she walked away with Violet. He smiled. At least he had one solid friend here in town. Hazel's kindness humbled him.

He swung his gaze around the café again. Joshua wasn't sure he wanted to socialize with any of the townsfolk. More important, he wasn't certain they had a single word to say to him. The past still stood between him and the town like a rushing river. In their eyes, he was responsible for burning down a beloved church. Although it hurt to be treated like a pariah, Joshua knew it was something most would find hard to forgive.

He looked around the establishment for his brother. Theo was on the other side of the room talking animatedly with some school friends. They were laughing and enjoying themselves. He felt a stab of jealousy. His brother didn't have the same target on his back as he did. In the town's eyes, Theo had been the accomplice the night of the fire. He hadn't been the fire starter. At moments such as this one, Joshua couldn't help but wish the truth had been told all those years ago. Being blamed for the fire had left him with scars he wasn't sure could ever be healed. If he had to do it all over again, he knew he wouldn't take the rap for the fire. It had cost him Honor's love—a price too high to bear.

"Joshua." Honor's honeyed voice flowed over him. He turned toward the sound of her. She was standing next to him looking gorgeous in a royal blue dress that made her blue-gray eyes pop. He hadn't seen her at the church, but it had overflowed with parishioners. It had pleased him to see so many people turn out to honor Bud.

"It was a lovely service. Bud would be proud."

"Thank you," he said. "Pastor Jack is a good man. He really knew my grandfather well." He let out a low chuckle. "Some of the stories he told were highly amusing. Sounded just like Bud."

"He'll be sorely missed. I was proud to call him my friend. He was very supportive of the wildlife center. He backed every single donor drive we held. And every now and again he would surprise me by popping up when I least expected it." A hint of a smile hovered on Honor's lips.

"Sounds like Gramps. Do you know he sent me a twenty-dollar bill in the mail every year for my birthday?"

Honor giggled. It sounded like music to his ears. It had been a long time since he'd heard the lovely sound. "That's really sweet."

Joshua had the sensation of eyes boring into him. Boone stood across the room, staring at him with an intensity Joshua couldn't ignore. He began to walk over toward where Joshua stood with Honor, his stride sure and steady. Honor eyed her brother warily.

Joshua met Boone's gaze head-on. Something told him Honor's brother hadn't walked over to offer condolences. Boone didn't waste any time. "I hear you've been talking to the Alloy Corporation about the Diamond R."

"That's right," Joshua said, his stare unwavering. A lot had changed in six years. He wasn't afraid of Sheriff Boone Prescott anymore. Back when he had been a teenager, Joshua had been intimidated by Boone's authority and the position he held in law enforcement. Not to mention the fact that he'd been Honor's big brother. Back then he had always been looking for trouble. Now, it was the last thing he wanted.

"Selling to that outfit will hurt this town," Boone said in a clipped tone. His voice was filled with censure.

"That remains to be seen," Joshua said. "It could open up the town to more revenue just like Lovely Boots," he said, referencing the boot company based on Hazel's creation of genuine Alaskan boots. From what his grandfather had told him, the company had helped Love put money back in the town coffers after years of downturn in the local economy.

"To be fair," Honor interjected, "Lovely Boots has provided a lot of jobs for locals. A dude ranch would largely benefit the owner. And it would make Love a tourist trap." Honor shuddered. "That would irrevocably change this town. It wouldn't be a quaint fishing village anymore. It would be unrecognizable."

Joshua bit back an angry retort. He counted to ten in his head before he responded. "A dude ranch would need employees, so it could help the local economy. Surely that's not a bad thing."

Honor didn't respond. Her jaw hardened. She had a mutinous expression stamped on her face.

She didn't need to say anything further. Of course Honor was siding with her brother. He shouldn't be surprised. Nothing had changed in this town. He was still on the outside looking in. But it didn't really matter what the Prescotts or the townsfolk thought. He and Theo had the authority to decide the destiny of the Diamond R Ranch. And there was nothing any of them could do about it. They held all the power. It was a complete reversal of fortune.

He didn't enjoy feeling this way, but for so long he had been powerless against the judgment and the condemnation of this small town. Even before the fire, Joshua had been viewed as a troublemaker and a rabble-rouser. His tarnished reputation had caused a lot of heartache for his mother, who had shed buckets of tears over the situation.

Suddenly, Cameron came over and stood next to Boone. Declan and Finn followed suit. Joshua let out a labored sigh. It was as if the cavalry had just ridden in. So much for a nice reception after Bud's memorial.

"So tell us, Ransom, is selling the ranch to the highest bidder a way of getting back at this town?" Cameron asked, his brows furrowed.

Joshua shook his head. He felt incredulous. Hadn't he established any goodwill in this town? He had lived here for eighteen years. Surely in all that time he'd done at least a few good things.

"For the record, revenge isn't my style," he said, keeping his voice calm and measured. Joshua didn't feel the need to explain that he had developed a relationship with God after leaving Love. He knew the God he served wouldn't want him to harbor hatred in his heart or fight with anyone. He had evolved over the past six years.

Provide things honest in the sight of all men. If it be possible, as much as lieth in you, live peaceably with all men.

Honor's face radiated discomfort. "Can you boys take it down a few notches?" Honor asked. "This isn't the time nor the place. Today is about Bud."

"Bud didn't want his land to be sold to someone who would desecrate it," Declan said. "It isn't what he wanted!"

"I'm getting pretty sick and tired of people telling me what my grandfather wanted!" Joshua gritted his teeth. "Let me just tell all of you at the same time so I won't have to repeat it. Nothing's been decided. Theo and I will take everything into consideration and decide what's best for us."

Finn shook his head. "That's no big surprise. Doing what's best for Love has never really interested you."

Joshua sucked his teeth. It was a low blow. His faith was being tested. *Turn the other cheek.* It was a Bible verse he lived by. But now there were people in his face pushing his buttons. There was only so much he could ignore.

Just then Theo walked up, nudging his way into the

circle. "What's going on over here?" he asked. "What did I miss? Are you guys catching up on old times?"

"Something like that," Joshua drawled, making eye contact with his brother.

"We were inquiring about your intention to sell the Diamond R," Boone explained. "Word has gotten around town. Folks are curious. And concerned about developers trampling all over Bud's land."

"That's mighty neighborly of you to ask," Theo said, grinning at Boone. "We're still weighing our options, but at the moment, selling to the Alloy Corporation is where we're leaning."

Boone scowled at Theo. The tension was so thick one could cut it with a knife.

Joshua could see the concern flickering in Honor's eyes. It was all over her face. She was dead set against the sale of the ranch and still reeling from disappointment about the provisions in Bud's will.

He felt a twisting sensation in his gut. So many years had passed by since they had been in love with one another, yet he still cared about what she thought of him. A part of him had secretly hoped Honor would be impressed by all the changes he'd undergone in the ensuing years. Clearly none of that mattered now. Her focus was on the Diamond R ranch and whether or not it would be turned into a trendy dude ranch.

Truth to be told, they were on opposite sides of the fence.

Despite what he had just said to Boone, Joshua's decision about the ranch had been made early this morning prior to Bud's memorial service. Theo had basically confirmed it just now. Bud's ranch would be sold. Joshua's life was in Seattle. He didn't need to hold on to anything here in Love. Once upon a time he had dreamed of settling down here with Honor, but all of those dreams had gone up in smoke. It was best that he cut all ties with the town that had made him an outcast. His grandfather's passing signified an end of an era.

Theo was right. Selling the ranch to the Alloy Corporation was the best choice they could make. He wasn't going to feel guilty about the decision. The money he would make on the deal would secure Violet's future. And it would permanently sever ties with a town that had never really embraced him.

Heat stained Honor's cheeks as she left the gathering and followed Boone into the kitchen. As soon as they were alone she tugged on her brother's arm and turned him around. "Was that really necessary?" Honor asked. "Why were you being so confrontational? We didn't need a scene at Bud's memorial reception."

Boone frowned at her. "Please don't take up for him. I thought six years would have given you some distance from the situation. I would hope you'd gained some objectivity."

She folded her arms across her chest. "I'm not defending him. Hazel arranged this reception. She went to a lot of trouble to do so. We all promised to respect her wishes. I think part of that meant not picking fights or rehashing old grudges."

Boone let out a snort. "He picked the fight six years ago."

"Don't make it personal," she cautioned. "I understand where you're coming from, but it doesn't serve any purpose."

He clenched his jaw. "He burned down the church

our folks got married in. We were all baptized there, all four of us. It doesn't get more personal than that," Boone said in a raised voice.

She let out a sigh. The fire that had gutted the church was still an emotional subject. In many ways, there hadn't been closure to the incident. It was like a scab that had never healed. So much had changed in her life after Joshua burned down the church. In her heart she had always believed it was accidental, but it still had been too much to forgive. There was no defending arson.

She had given Joshua his ring back and headed to college in Michigan at Boone's urging. He had wanted her to get as far away from her ex-fiancé as possible. Although she had initially been angry at her brother for forcing her hand, she'd been grateful to him in the long run.

Tears pooled in her eyes. A tightening sensation spread across her chest. "I know what he did, Boone. Why is it that you always seem to forget what I lost? I was engaged to him. He was my high school sweetheart. I loved him. So I understand you were devastated about the church, but for me it was like a tsunami effect. I lost my entire world!"

Boone reached out and pulled her into his arms. He cradled her against his chest and patted her back in a soothing motion. "I'm sorry, Honor. I let my temper get the best of me. You know I never liked Joshua. I didn't think for a single second he was good enough for you."

Still, after all this time, it hurt to hear Boone talk about Joshua in such a negative way. "But he was good," she insisted. "I realize you never approved of him. I know he caused trouble and he ran wild all over town. You took him into custody more times than I can count. But there were great qualities about him as well. He was kind. Loyal. Sweet. Funny. He treated me well." Her voice began to quiver as thoughts of her ex-fiancé came into sharp focus. "So for me, it's always been hard to judge him by his worst moments when there were so many others along the way."

Boone cupped her chin in his hand. "Honor Prescott, you're a good woman. You believe in people. Sometimes too much. I believe in forgiveness, but when it comes to Joshua I have a hard time with it." He pressed a kiss against her temple. "I'm sorry about earlier. The thought of this town turning into a tourist's haven is weighing heavily on me."

"I know. Me too. It would be a nightmare," she said. "But I'm not giving up on the idea of the Ransom brothers deciding not to sell. It's their birthright after all. Maybe they'll change their minds."

A hint of a smile twitched at Boone's lips. "There you go again with your pie-in-the-sky thinking. It's one of the things I love most about you. You're idealistic." A sigh slipped past his lips. "I hate to break it to you, but Theo and Joshua haven't lived here in quite some time, nor have they been back to visit. What makes you think they harbor warm and fuzzy feelings about Bud's ranch? I think Theo was giving it to us straight. They're selling." His mouth was set in grim lines.

Honor opened her mouth, then shut it. How could she dispute Boone's assessment of the situation? He was right. Theo had pretty much confirmed it. In all likelihood, Joshua would accept a big fat check for the sale of the ranch, then head back to Seattle where he belonged. But she was still going to hold on to a kernel of hope. Joshua had always loved the ranch. It was hard to imagine him selling it.

Her sister-in-law Grace popped her head in the kitchen and regarded them both with a wary expression. "Is everything all right in here?" she asked.

"Everything is fine," Honor said, reaching up and pressing a kiss on her brother's cheek. No matter if they disagreed from time to time, Honor adored her older brother. He, along with her grandfather, had raised her in the absence of their parents. He had always wanted the best for her. She hadn't always been able to see it or appreciate his overprotectiveness, but at this point in her life she knew Boone had led with his heart. No doubt he would do the same with his own daughter.

"Good," Grace said with a grin. "We should probably get going. Eva is fading fast. Jasper's holding her right now and he's telling her stories about her ancestors searching for gold in the Yukon."

Boone shook his head and laughed. "Uh-oh. We better go rescue her."

Honor watched as Boone grabbed a hold of Grace's hand and headed back toward the main area of the café. She felt a little bereft. Watching as other couples happily settled down was getting harder and harder for Honor. She always felt joyful for them, but increasingly she was feeling more and more alone.

What was wrong with her? Why didn't she feel a pressing need to get out there and find love? She was lonely at times and secretly yearning for a perfect match. How amazing would it be if she could find her other half like Liam or Boone, or Jasper and Cameron? Or any other number of couples here in town?

Love one another. Wasn't that God's command?

These emotions always struck her whenever she attended a town event where residents were coupled up. And in a town where Operation Love was in full force, it was hard to avoid romance. It was as if there was this little hole inside her aching to be filled up. Despite what she tried to tell herself—that she wasn't looking for love—Honor knew it was the great big lie of her life. She tended to stuff all of the emotions down so she didn't have to face them. It wasn't working anymore. Those needs were bubbling to the surface.

She shook off the morose thoughts. There was a much more pressing matter at hand. If no one intervened, it was very likely the Diamond R would be sold to a developer. The very idea of it made her sick to her stomach. Feelings of helplessness washed over her. She didn't like being in this frame of mind. Surely something could be done to mediate the situation?

What if she invited Joshua to the wildlife center and showed him what a wonderful haven it was for rescued animals? Perhaps he would see how vital it was to preserve precious Alaskan land. The very land the wildlife center sat on had been given to the town by a resident—Miss Mary Mae Pritchard—in her will. If Mary had sold to a developer, the center wouldn't even exist, nor would the animals have been rescued.

Preserving wildlife and keeping the land intact went hand in hand in Honor's estimation. With the Diamond R bordering the wildlife's property, Honor knew a dude ranch would impact her own way of life. The very thought of it made her feel uncomfortable. Perhaps she could sway Joshua to her way of thinking, or at the very least get him to see a different point of view.

It was a long shot, but Honor truly believed it was

possible to change hearts and minds. It was a big part of her faith. Things had gotten out of hand earlier between the Ransom brothers and her own siblings. That wasn't Honor's way. If it was possible, she wanted to try to smooth things over. Like Hazel always said, you could catch more bees with honey than with vinegar. Honor was about to test out that theory with Joshua.

She prayed it wouldn't be too difficult to spend time alone with Joshua Ransom and his adorable baby girl. Hopefully it wouldn't serve as a reminder of everything she'd lost in the past.

Chapter Five

It was a perfect February Alaskan afternoon for a trip to the wildlife center. The sky was as blue as a robin's egg. Although there was snow on the ground and a chill in the air, it was spectacular weather for this time of year. Joshua had bundled Violet up in a snowsuit, hat and mittens. He tended to be overprotective of his daughter. At three months' old she'd contracted bronchitis, which had led to a three-day stay in the hospital. Joshua hadn't left her side for a single moment.

He buckled her into her car seat and tested it to make sure it was secure. Parenthood wasn't for the faint of heart. Violet twisted his heart up like a pretzel. He had never felt like this before in his life. Well, just once, he corrected himself. Honor used to make him feel as if he could soar like an eagle just by looking in his direction. His pulse began to race as he thought about those days. It had been so long ago, yet he remembered every moment as if it were yesterday.

Joshua had been floored by Honor's invitation to visit the wildlife center. If it hadn't been for Violet, he might have declined. Even though she was too young to fully absorb the experience, Joshua still liked to expose his daughter to the world around her. The truth was, Honor still caused his heart to beat a little faster whenever he was in her presence. He wasn't in love with her anymore, but he still felt a tug in her direction. Perhaps it was the abrupt way their relationship had ended. One moment they had been planning to get married and settle down in Love, while in the next Honor was giving back his ring and leaving town to attend college out of state. If he lived to be one hundred, Joshua would never forget the look of hurt and disillusionment in her eyes when she had ended things after finding out about the fire.

He had asked himself the same questions hundreds of times. What if he hadn't taken the blame for the fire? Would he have ridden off into the sunset with Honor? Would they be building a family and working together on their life goals at this very moment?

He shook off the futile questions. One thing he knew for certain. If he hadn't taken a certain path, Violet wouldn't be in his life now. And without his daughter, life didn't really make much sense. She gave him a purpose each and every day. Some might say he had saved her from being an orphan, but in truth, Violet had been the best thing to ever happen to him. She infused his life with colors. Reds. Oranges. Vivid purples. He made sure to thank God each day for making him a father.

As he settled into the driver's seat and began to make his way to the wildlife center, the stunning Alaskan vista came into view. The spectacular view of the mountains always left him in awe. Tall, snow-covered trees dominated the landscape. Hawks flew gracefully up in the sky, dipping down every now and again, then soaring back toward the heavens.

Although many residents of Love preferred to live near town, Joshua had always enjoyed living out in the boondocks. It was serene out here. Nothing but the great outdoors and breathtaking views of Alaska.

As soon as he saw the sign for the wildlife center, Joshua turned down the road and followed the arrows. Before he knew it, he had arrived at a ranch-style house surrounded by several small, flat structures. He could see horses running in a paddock in the distance.

By the time he parked Bud's truck and got Violet out of her car seat, Honor was walking toward them from a nearby building. With her hair pulled away from her face in a high ponytail, she looked like a fresh-faced beauty. She wasn't wearing a hint of makeup, and she was dressed casually in a pair of blue jeans and a navy blue parka. A gray wool hat sat on her head. To this day, Honor was the loveliest woman he'd ever seen.

This invitation to the center had come as a complete surprise, especially after the tension that had flared up between him and her family at Bud's reception.

She waved at them. "Hey, Joshua. Glad you could make it out here."

He nodded at her. "Thanks for the invitation. I thought it would be good for Violet to experience a little bit of my hometown. When she's older I can tell her all about how she visited Love."

Honor smiled at Violet, who turned away and hid her face against his chest. "She's a bit shy at first. It'll take her a few minutes to come around."

"I don't blame her one bit," Honor said in a cheery voice. "After all, I'm basically a stranger to her. And she's here in this new town where she doesn't really know anybody. It's a lot for her to absorb all at once."

He felt grateful for Honor's understanding of the situation. It was hard for Violet to be away from home and trying to acclimate to her new surroundings. The past few nights she had awoken in the wee hours of the morning crying out for him.

"Well, she's at a good age for an introduction to animals. I promise we won't visit any that might frighten her."

"I appreciate it," Joshua said. "She spooks easily, although she loves animals. She's really enjoying the horses at the ranch. Her favorite place back home is the zoo."

Joshua knew he was probably telling Honor way more than she wanted to know, but things still felt a bit awkward between them. They had once had such a familiarity between them, with conversation flowing as effortlessly as a river. But now, with years stretched out between them, he was searching for something to say. He prayed the awkwardness would melt away.

"Zoos are wonderful places to engage children and educate them about animals. I'll never forget my first visit to the Alaska Zoo when I was six years old. It changed my life. From that point forward, I knew what I wanted to do with the rest of my life." Her voice rang out with conviction.

"I've been meaning to say congratulations on all of this," Joshua said. He swung his gaze around the area, amazed by the scope of it. Dragging his eyes away from Honor took effort. She was extremely pleasing to the eye.

"Thanks," she said. "I didn't get here on my own.

Boone and Jasper really helped me with tuition. I received a partial scholarship, but there was still a chunk I had to pay. It wasn't easy, but I held a few part-time jobs to help with the bills. It was a big financial sacrifice for my family, so I wanted to pay for all the incidentals on my own."

It shouldn't matter after all these years, but it still rankled that Boone had orchestrated Honor's moving away to Michigan to attend college. For a long time, he had wondered whether they would have gotten back together if she hadn't left Love so abruptly. Michigan had been so far away and there hadn't been a single way for him to contact her. In the aftermath of their breakup, she had changed her email address and her cell phone number. All avenues had been closed to him since she wasn't active on social media.

It was all water under the bridge now. He had made his peace with all of it a long time ago.

"I wouldn't expect any less from our class valedictorian," he said in a teasing tone. Honor had been the top student in their high school class. She had deserved a scholarship to an excellent university and a pathway to the career of her dreams. It probably wouldn't have worked out if they had both stayed in Love and been married as teens. It would have been yet another mistake.

"You weren't exactly a slouch yourself," she answered. "You were a great student when you weren't goofing off."

They both chuckled, enjoying a moment where they could reflect on the past with frivolity and not bitterness. There had been so many wonderful moments shared between them. Even though he had tried to convince himself otherwise, their love had been real. It just hadn't been built to last.

"Why don't we go take a look at the horses?" Honor suggested. "They're very gentle, and Violet might get a kick out of petting them."

"Let's go," Joshua said, walking beside Honor as she led them toward the paddock. Violet's eyes grew wide as they reached the horses. She couldn't seem to take her eyes off them. She pointed a chubby finger in the direction of a butterscotch-colored Palomino.

"Ba Ba," she said, reaching out to touch the stallion.

"I think she likes him," Joshua said, allowing Violet to pat the horse's side. He knew better than to let her put her hands by the horse's mouth. When Joshua was a kid, Bud had taught him how to stay safe around horses.

"She has good taste," Honor raved. "That's Pecan. She's a real sweetheart. She was my first rescue and rehabilitation. I wasn't certain she would make it at first." Honor visibly shuddered. "She was in really bad shape. Neglected and abused. Ultimately, our goal is for people to adopt the horses, but I've decided to keep Pecan. She holds a special place in my heart. Just like Lola."

Lola had been Honor's horse ever since her thirteenth birthday.

"How many do you have at the moment?" he asked.

"About twenty-five or so. We have some wild mustangs that just came to us. They're magnificent horses but they have some injuries that would make it impossible to be out on their own. So we're rehabilitating them."

Joshua let out a low whistle. "Please tell me you're not doing this all by yourself."

"No way. That would be tough. I have two full-time workers and a few part-timers who come in as needed. We're all really hands-on since the whole point of the center is to provide a safe, nurturing environment for animals who've been in precarious situations."

"This place is impressive," he said with a nod. "It's nice to see you making a difference in the community. I know it's what you always wanted to do."

She brushed her chestnut locks away from her face. "I consider myself very blessed. Not many people get to work in their dream job."

Violet's shyness faded away after a short amount of time in Honor's presence. She couldn't take her eyes off the animals. Or Honor. Joshua suspected his daughter found Honor fascinating because she herself didn't have a mother. There really weren't too many female figures in her life. Although Joshua had always dreamed of having a wife and kids, he didn't think he was very good at relationships. He'd reconciled himself to the idea of raising Violet as a single dad even though he knew finding a wife would be a dream come true. The thing was, he still couldn't seem to reconcile the word *wife* with anyone but Honor. It was probably one of the reasons his marriage to Lauren had failed.

"Do you still ride?" she asked.

"Not regularly," he admitted. "Riding isn't big in Seattle. It's a large, bustling city."

"I'm surprised to hear that. You loved riding more than anyone I've ever known, including Bud. You were the quintessential Alaskan cowboy."

Honor was right. It had been a huge part of his life. "Those were the days. I miss it," he said, his eyes straying toward the horses in the paddock. "I never felt more like myself than when I was on horseback. I don't know how to put it into words, but sometimes it seemed as if I was one with the horse."

"Spoken like a true horseman. You miss the ranch," she said, a knowing look glinting from her eyes. "I know what it meant to you. You and Bud were an amazing team. Two peas in a pod."

"I never imagined I'd leave," he said in a wistful tone. "In the end I didn't really have a choice, did I?"

"Not really," she said in a soft voice. "Considering everything, it was for the best."

The best? It stung a little hearing Honor felt that way about his exile from Love. It had been the most agonizing period of his life. He was probably being overly sensitive, but he wondered if he'd been wrong after all. Maybe Honor had never really loved him.

"It came out the wrong way," she blurted out. "It sounded harsh, but I didn't mean to sound so cavalier. Bud probably never told you, but things were really tense around here after the fire. People were really up in arms. I remember hearing Boone say if you had stuck around there could have been retaliation against you."

He jammed a hand through his hair. "I'm not surprised. Tensions were running high before I left town," Joshua said. "Bud never said a word about it though. I hated it for him. It makes me angry he had to suffer for our actions."

"Bud was tough. He could handle all the backlash. He was also beloved in this town. The majority of residents had his back."

Warmth settled over him at the idea of his grandfather being supported by the residents. He had deserved no less. Bud Ransom had been a wonderful person.

"So, where did you go when you left Love?" Honor asked. "I was at school, but I heard a lot of things through the grapevine." She began to giggle, then placed her hand over her mouth. "It's not funny, but rumors were running rampant about your whereabouts. Someone even surmised you'd joined the traveling circus."

Joshua burst out laughing. Never in a million years had he ever thought he'd laugh over the circumstances of his expulsion from town. But, as in the past, Honor had the ability to make him chuckle.

"After completing the first-time offender program, I traveled with my parents. My dad got an assignment overseas. So I was in Singapore for a year. I took some business classes and stretched myself."

Honor's eyes widened. "Wow. Singapore? That's impressive. And here I imagined you were sitting in a dungeon somewhere."

Joshua met her gaze. He sensed her comment was on the passive-aggressive side. Did she think he hadn't suffered? "I didn't get off scot-free in case you were wondering. I had to pay restitution in addition to what Bud paid to repair the church."

"You were fortunate to have Bud in your corner." She avoided looking at him. Instead she reached out and fiddled with Violet's fingers. He heard a slight edge to her tone. Joshua felt a nagging sensation inside him. Honor was still harboring negative feelings from the past. Did she believe he had put his grandfather in a bad position?

Suddenly, he felt guilty all over again. He hated feeling this way. How long would he have to beat himself up over the choices he'd made? Was it a life sentence?

He cleared his throat.

"Honor, you've been gracious to me and Violet. I know most folks here in town wrote me off a long time ago. They've been cordial only because I'm Bud's grandson. You didn't have to invite us over here today, especially considering everything that went down between us in the past."

Her hair swung about her shoulders as she shook her head. "We've both moved on from all that, Joshua. We were kids back then."

Kids. He hated the way she phrased it, as if they hadn't known what they were doing. In reality, they had been very much in love and committed to a life together. Their dedication to each other had been heartwarming, although being intimate with Honor had been a huge mistake. Since that time, Joshua had turned his life over to the Lord. He now knew how wrong their actions had been.

He shook off his irritation with Honor. "It's only fair that I give you a heads-up. The bottom line is that Theo and I have decided to sell the ranch. It's really the only sensible thing for us to do." He pushed the words past his lips before he could chicken out.

A look of shock passed over her face. The lines of her mouth hardened. She raised an eyebrow. "Sensible? That's hardly a word I'd choose to describe what you and Theo are planning to do."

Something about her disappointed expression made Joshua want to reach out and hold her in his arms. It was a reflex from back in the day. He had always strived to soothe Honor's wounds. It was no longer his job to do so, no matter how much he might want to at this moment.

"I know it's not happy news. But, to be honest, we're between a rock and a hard place. Love hasn't been our home for quite some time. We're only passing through town, so to speak. Our lives are elsewhere."

She frowned at him. "Jasper has an expression. You can try as best you can to run away from home, but it's always going to be a part of you."

"I agree with you, Honor. To an extent. And I'm not running away from anything this time. I'm walking toward something. A home for Violet and me. Security. A place where she's always going to know she's loved. We have a great life in Seattle."

Who was he trying to convince? He was making it sound way more idyllic than it really was. But he was being truthful about this town. Love hadn't been home in quite some time.

Honor bowed her head. "And what about the ranch? Can you really just walk away from it, knowing the Diamond R is going to cease to exist as you know it? Can you live with that?" she pressed.

He glanced down at his daughter. Violet was rubbing her eyes and fading fast. In Joshua's opinion, it was the perfect moment to head back to the Diamond R. Honor had been kind and solicitous, but tensions were rising. He didn't want things to completely fall apart. It was best to end things in a civil manner.

"We've made up our minds," he said in a firm voice. "I don't expect everyone to agree with us, but I hope our decision will be respected."

"Well, then," Honor said in a crisp voice. "I guess there's nothing more to be said." Honor's tone spoke volumes. Her voice crackled with anger. There was no mistaking the look of fury on her face.

He shifted Violet to his hip. She had fallen asleep against his chest. Violet was getting heavier by the day. No doubt she was going through a growth spurt.

Maybe coming here today had been a mistake.

The civil mood between him and Honor had deteriorated. Perhaps both of them had just been going through the motions. The air between them was thick with tension. "We should get going. I need to run into town to get a few things for Violet. Thanks for having us over here, even though I'm beginning to think you had an agenda."

Honor stood with her arms folded across her chest. She appeared slightly shocked and wounded.

"I hoped to talk some sense into you, but clearly I overestimated your ability to see beyond your own needs and wants. I thought you might consider Bud's legacy and the integrity of this town." Her voice quivered with emotion. He could see the pain radiating from her eyes.

He hated himself for hurting her, but there was no point in sugarcoating the situation about the Diamond R. She would have found out sooner or later anyway. Joshua was done living his life for others. He had a responsibility to provide a wonderful life for his daughter. There was no way he could ever do that here in Love where the townsfolk viewed him as a ne'er do well. He didn't owe them anything! Not after the way they had treated him like yesterday's trash.

He turned toward his vehicle and opened up the door. If he looked into her eyes, he just might break in two. Honor stayed silent until he'd buckled Violet into her car seat and settled himself behind the wheel.

"Don't do it. Don't sell! You'll regret it, Joshua," she called out after him. "It's Bud's legacy you would be selling. It's something you can never replace in a million years."

Joshua turned and looked at her from his position in the driver's seat. He hated seeing her so broken up about the ranch, but there was nothing he could do to change things. He didn't bother to respond to her. Joshua revved the engine and drove away from the wildlife center, his soul feeling wearier than it had felt in recent memory. Why, after all this time, did Honor Prescott still have such sway over his emotions? Why did she always make him question the things he thought he knew with a deep certainty?

Honor's words rang in his ears well after he reached the ranch and settled Violet down for a nap.

Don't do it. Don't sell! You'll regret it, Joshua.

Honor couldn't seem to move from the spot she had been standing in when Joshua had roared off in Bud's truck with Violet.

We've made up our minds.

Theo and I have decided to sell the ranch.

Honor couldn't shake her conversation with Joshua. She couldn't believe the words that had tumbled out of his mouth. Her stomach clenched as feelings of betrayal washed over her. Tears of frustration pooled in her eyes. What a fool she had been to believe Joshua would be swayed by her words!

They were selling the ranch! Bud's beloved Diamond R would be transformed into a commercial enterprise. If only Bud had protected his land by making certain his will mirrored his wishes. In her heart Honor hadn't really believed Joshua would be capable of moving forward with the sale. He had always been sentimental about the ranch. Who was this version of the young man she had thought she'd known like the back of her hand?

She felt so hopeless. Her grand plan to convince Joshua to reconsider his position had been a huge flop. He had already made up his mind before he'd stepped foot on the grounds of the nature preserve.

Honor bit her lip. She wasn't a helpless person. She was smart and resourceful. And she believed in this town and the Alaskan environment more than mere words could express.

What if she could figure out a way to prevent the sale of the Diamond R Ranch? What if there was a legal way to stop Joshua and Theo from selling to the Alloy Corporation? Lee had said it wasn't possible to challenge Bud's will. But what if there was a way around it? Something tied in to land preservation. She saw it all the time in the news where people fought against construction in rural areas.

As town mayor, Jasper might be aware of some technicality by which the sale of the land to developers could be challenged. She needed to be certain before she crossed this bridge. Once she headed down this road, there would be no turning back. Joshua would no doubt be angry at her for interfering, but Honor felt strongly about the situation. She would be acting for a higher purpose than the Ransom brothers. Clearly, all they cared about was the almighty dollar.

In this case, the ends justified the means. As an animal rehabilitator and land preservationist, she couldn't bear it if strangers descended on her beloved town and started digging up the land. Having hordes of tourists stomping around Jarvis Street would ruin the town's laid-back vibe. It wasn't just sour grapes about Bud not leaving the land to the town. It was about principles. It was about keeping Love quaint and pristine.

If she had to go head-to-head with the Ransom brothers in order to protect her hometown, that's just what Honor intended to do.

Chapter Six

Joshua stood outside the paddock and gazed at the wide array of horses that had belonged to Bud. Chocolate. Midnight black. Sienna. Bone white. He had always been fascinated by the vast array of colors horses came in. These animals were an integral part of the Diamond R Ranch. A huge lover of horses, Bud Ransom had been proud to call himself a cowboy and a rancher. Gramps had been the one to teach Joshua how to ride when he was five years old. Joshua had fallen in love with horses and with the Diamond R Ranch.

It had been a long time since he had been home, but he was falling in love with it all over again. With each and every day he was falling into old, familiar rhythms and seeing his hometown with fresh eyes.

He had just now ridden across the property on Blaze, his grandfather's favorite horse. He wasn't sure how it had happened over the years, but he had forgotten how wonderful it felt to fly like the wind on a prized stallion's back. It brought back a part of him he had thought was gone forever. The carefree boy who had dreamed of being a cattle rancher and owning his own spread. There wasn't much riding for him in Seattle due to his hectic work schedule. Getting a business off the ground and raising a child consumed most of his time.

It was a nice change of pace to hang out with the horses.

Pride soared through him as he swung his gaze around the ranch. The property stretched out for miles. Pure Alaskan land. He felt a twinge of regret over his decision to sell the ranch. Theo had worked overtime to convince him of the wisdom of selling rather than holding on to the property for nostalgic reasons. He hadn't told Honor, but he'd been on the fence regarding the decision. Much like the way he'd done in childhood, Theo had pushed him over the edge regarding the sale.

If he closed his eyes he could picture himself as his pint-sized self, following after Bud as he walked around the Diamond R. He'd been his grandfather's shadow, wanting to know everything he could about running a ranch.

He scoffed. What was he being sentimental for? It wasn't possible to keep the Diamond R. It wasn't as if either he or Theo wanted to establish roots here in Love. Been there, done that. Nobody really wanted them to stay anyway. They just wanted his family's land.

He heard the whir of tires crunching on the snow and turned in the direction of the road. It was Theo. He had headed into town earlier in order to meet with Eric Mathers, Bud's attorney. Joshua had been content to stay back at the ranch while Theo sorted through the paperwork regarding their inheritance. Violet was inside the house with Winnie, the Ransom housekeeper.

She had cheerfully agreed to watch the baby while he poked around the ranch.

Theo drove right up to the stables, then stopped on a dime. Joshua frowned. His brother had gotten out of the car and was making his way toward him. His stride was full of anger.

So much for his peaceful morning. Instinct told him things were about to take a turn for the worse.

"What's going on? Are you all right? You look like a storm cloud," he called out to Theo as he approached.

"You're not going to believe it!" he announced from a few feet away. His face was twisted up in anger. His eyes flashed warning signs.

"Maybe you need to take a few deep breaths," Joshua said. "You don't look so good."

Theo stopped right in front of Joshua. He was breathing heavily. A vein bulged over his eye.

"We've been stopped in our tracks, Joshua. We can't move forward in selling the ranch. An injunction was filed preventing us from selling to the Alloy Corporation. Eric said that an argument is being made that the property should be blocked from sale to any developers."

"An injunction? On what grounds?" he asked. His mind raced with the impact of the news. This had Boone written all over it. In his eyes, Joshua would always be the villain. He had probably jumped at the opportunity to make trouble for him. No doubt he wouldn't be content until he left Love forever.

"An argument was made that since the land borders the wildlife preserve, it's federally protected land. Since some of those animals are endangered, construction could hamper their ability to thrive."

Joshua's jaw dropped. It was a slick move, designed to put a wrench in their plans. He wasn't sure if the argument had merit, but it would surely grind things to a halt. "Sounds like they threw whatever they thought might stick against the wall."

Theo jammed his hands into his back pockets. "Yes. I think you're right. Now a judge has to decide on the matter. It really messes things up for us. The Alloy Corporation might not want all this hassle and legal wrangling. And it's going to cost us a small fortune if it's litigated."

Litigation! This could seriously affect both of them financially. He didn't have money to defend lawsuits!

"I can't believe Boone would go to those lengths," Joshua muttered. He was well aware of the sheriff's ill will toward him, but he'd never imagined Boone would resort to filing legal papers to impede them. This situation had truly spiraled out of control.

"It wasn't Boone. Matter of fact it wasn't any of the Prescott men. Or the O'Rourkes." Theo chewed on the inside of his lip. "It was none other than your ex-fiancée, Honor Prescott."

Honor? Theo must have gotten his information wrong. There was no way Honor would go the route of filing an injunction against them.

"No. That doesn't sound right," Joshua said, shaking his head in disbelief. Sweet, kind Honor. "She wouldn't do such a thing."

Theo twisted his mouth. "Yes, actually she would. And she did! That's exactly what Eric told me. She filed legal paperwork to impede our sale of the ranch. She's citing imminent harm to the animals at the wildlife preserve."

A fierce anger raced through Joshua's veins. She had used the information he had given her the other day regarding selling the ranch to try to undermine them. Who did Honor think she was to tie their hands in such a manner? This was a spiteful act. Honor had never been a vindictive person. Was this payback for the past? Bitterness over the will? Or just a way to let him know he had no business here in town. If so, he wasn't just going to roll over and play dead.

"Can you let Winnie know I need her to watch Violet for another hour or so?" Joshua asked.

Theo frowned at him. "Where are you going?"

"To the wildlife center. It's about time I got a few things straight with Honor."

Theo called out after him, imploring him to come back. Joshua didn't heed his brother's pleas. He strode off toward the direction of Bud's truck, feeling grateful the keys were in the ignition. He didn't want to have to go back inside the house and allow Violet to see him like this.

His youthful years had been full of swagger and rage. As a grown man he had made a conscious effort to be even-tempered and calm. In many ways, his past troubles had been a result of his inability to control his temper.

Let every man be swift to hear, slow to speak, slow to wrath. In his estimation, it was one of the most powerful Bible verses. It had always resonated with him.

At this very moment, Joshua knew his anger was beyond anything he'd experienced in adulthood. A part of him felt like the wild, reckless boy of his youth. The feelings surprised him. He'd been of the belief that he had gotten rid of that boy a long time ago. But Honor had pressed every last one of his buttons by embroiling him and Theo in a legal battle. He felt like a volcano that was about to blow sky-high.

Honor held a baby lynx in her arms and firmly placed the bottle in her mouth. She grinned as Glory greedily guzzled the milk. The baby lynx was finally showing signs of thriving. She had rejected food for days, raising alarm bells with Honor. Seeing Glory eating caused a feeling of triumph to surge up inside her. For all intents and purposes, Honor was serving the role of mother. Honor wrinkled her nose. Some might find it silly, but she loved her ability to mother and nurture the animals. It filled up an emotional void in her life.

It filled, she realized, her own yearning for motherhood. Ever since laying eyes on Violet, her own loss had been pressing on her heart. She still mourned the loss of her child. Sometimes, in the still hours between darkness and dawn, she thought about what might have been.

The quiet of the center settled around her like a warm, cozy blanket. It was such an idyllic setting. It was a great place to listen to her own thoughts as they rambled around her brain. It was important, especially in the past few days.

As someone who had grown up in a big, bustling family like her own, it was a wonder she didn't mind the isolation of the wildlife center. There was something calm and peaceful about being out here with all of the animals. She loved what she did for a living. It had been worth all the years of being in Michigan away from her loved ones. Running the wildlife center was a dream come true. She still wasn't sure what she had done in this lifetime to receive such a blessing.

Heavy footsteps sounded in the distance. Perhaps it was Clay Mathers, one of the workers. He didn't usually stomp around the place though. She turned toward the door, watching as it swung open with a loud crashing sound.

Joshua stood there, all six feet of him, bristling with a ferocious anger. It radiated from him in waves. His blue eyes glittered with animosity. Honor shuddered. She had never in her life seen Joshua look at her with such condemnation in his eyes. Even at his worst, he had always gazed at her with love radiating from his eyes. It was a bit unsettling to see this version of Joshua.

"What do you think you're doing?" Joshua demanded.

"You need to lower your voice. I'm trying to get her to sleep," Honor said, placing her finger to her lips in a shushing motion.

Joshua's face hardened. "I need to talk to you. Now!"

"I know why you're here," she said in a loud whisper. "And I'm very sorry if you're upset with me, but I had to take action before you sold the ranch."

"No, you didn't," he said in a low voice. "You could have just let things be instead of meddling. This doesn't concern you."

She glared at him. "Meddling? I'm doing my civic duty for this town."

"It's not your business!" he spit out. "It's Ransom land."

She sat up straight. "It is my business. I'm from this town. Love flows in my veins. I could no sooner turn my back on the fate of this town than I could forsake my own family. And Bud wouldn't want this. Someone needs to speak for him! It's his legacy you're keen on destroying."

Joshua scoffed. "So now that you're a wildlife biologist you're suddenly saving the world from developers? Riding to the rescue? Is that it?"

"I have principles that guide me," she said. "I always have."

He threw his hands in the air. "You're affecting my future by what you're doing. And Violet's. How could you do that?"

"It's not about you, Joshua. It's about this town. The people. We deserve better than to have developers come in and twist Love into something it isn't and can never be. Doesn't that bother you?" she asked in a voice choked with emotion. "Don't you feel sad about the idea of Bud's beautiful ranch being turned into something ridiculous and frivolous? A dude ranch," she sneered. "It's utter nonsense."

"When did you become so judgmental?" he asked. "When did you appoint yourself as judge, jury and executioner?"

She jutted out her chin. "Probably around the same time you became so money hungry. Let's face it, there's only one reason you're considering this offer from the Alloy Corporation. And it has to do with you and Theo fattening up your bank balances. You're selling out for cold, hard cash."

"Do you know what I think?" Joshua asked, taking a step closer to her. "I think you've been spending too much time around your brothers and Jasper. They've rubbed off on you. You never used to be cynical. Or coldhearted."

"I wonder why?" She asked. "You made me more jaded than all my family members combined."

He frowned at her. "So is that what this is about? Settling old scores? Getting even with me?"

"Clearly you think I have no integrity. I'm not doing this for personal reasons."

Joshua narrowed his gaze as he studied her. "So it has nothing to do with any lingering feelings you might have for me?"

Honor sucked in a shocked breath. She couldn't believe what Joshua was insinuating. What had she done to make him believe she was harboring residual feelings for him? She met his gaze head-on. "Everything I ever felt for you died the moment you lit the church on fire."

She could see the hurt in his eyes. He tried to shake it off, but she had seen the glint of pain before it disappeared and he shuttered his expression.

"We're going to fight you on this, Honor. And we'll win. You don't have a leg to stand on. If you really love this town, you might want to think about it before you drag it through a very expensive legal case." Joshua's words hung in the air like a thinly veiled threat.

He turned on his booted heels and left the building. Moments later she heard the engine of a vehicle revving up. She let out a shudder. Going head-to-head with Joshua had been painful. But she had no one to blame but herself. She had served the first volley by going to Jasper and working with him and Lee to get papers filed against the sale of the Diamond R.

She felt bad about the animosity between them, but she wasn't going to crumble into dust. Years ago she had been defenseless against Joshua. She'd been so naive and trusting. His actions had made a fool of her after all the lengths she'd gone to in order to defend him to her family and the townsfolk. He had shattered her belief in him with one horrific act. All of her dreams of marrying him and building a life together had evaporated. She had been left with nothing but pain and regret. Discovering she had been pregnant with their child and then losing the baby had been devastating.

Being vulnerable to Joshua had never served her well. She had vowed to herself a long time ago to never allow herself such weakness again. Dealing with her ex-fiancé meant hardening her heart against him. Joshua Ransom knew how to worm his way into her good graces like no one else.

She couldn't afford to let that happen. Loving and losing Joshua had already torn her world apart once before. Honor was going to focus on making sure the Diamond R wasn't turned into a tacky dude ranch. She couldn't afford to consider Joshua's feelings or picture Violet's angelic little face. If she did, Honor knew she would be in a world of trouble.

Chapter Seven

Joshua sat back in the leather love seat in the living room and sighed in contentment. His hands were resting behind his head while his feet were perched on the matching ottoman. The only sounds were coming from Violet, who was happily playing with her toys. He had set out a large blanket and scattered her favorite playthings around so she could explore them to her heart's content. He got a kick out of watching her scoot around.

They had the house all to themselves this evening. Theo was reconnecting with an old friend here in town while Winnie was spending the evening with her own family. Joshua enjoyed the silence. Quiet moments with his daughter meant the world to him. He had never imagined fatherhood would be his most sacred role. Violet had given his life a true purpose. He was no longer searching for meaning. God had been good to him.

And it hardly ever crossed his mind that his blood didn't flow in Violet's veins. It simply didn't matter. The love he felt for her came straight from the deepest parts of his soul.

The lights began to flicker for the third time this evening. Joshua frowned. He needed to locate the lanterns and flashlights in case they lost power. Although he had looked around earlier, he'd been unsuccessful in finding anything. He had a vague memory of Bud going down to the basement after a power outage and coming back with an armful of supplies. He unfolded himself from his comfy chair and stretched.

"I'll be right back, Vi. I need to make sure we have some flashlights and supplies in case the lights go out." His daughter just looked at him and gurgled, then went back to playing with her doll. Joshua quickly moved toward the hallway and yanked open the basement door. He flipped the light switch, bathing the darkened basement in light. He walked down the steps and began poking around in bins and drawers. Bingo! A whole drawer full of flashlights! The lanterns had to be around here somewhere.

Suddenly, the silence in the basement was broken. He heard a succession of loud thumps as if something had fallen. For a moment, he completely froze. Fear grabbed him by the throat. When he heard the loud cries, he pivoted toward the steps. Violet was lying at the bottom, her features contorted in pain. Her loud wails pierced his heart. He raced to her side, murmuring words of comfort.

Joshua gently scooped his daughter up in his arms and brought her back upstairs. With his free hand he reached for his car keys, wallet and cell phone. There was no question in his mind that she needed immediate medical attention. All could he do at the moment was pray that Violet wasn't too seriously injured.

* * *

As far as Saturday nights in Love, Alaska, went, hot chocolate and s'mores before a roaring fire at the Moose Café was a rip-roaring good time. Honor sighed. She truly loved her hometown, but every now and again she yearned to kick up her heels. For the most part, Honor worked at the wildlife center and watched as everyone else in town settled down to domestic bliss. With each couple that paired off, it became harder and harder to tell herself she was fine being single and unattached.

Dear Lord, one of these days, I would like to find someone who'll sweep me off my feet. I haven't been ready to plunge into the dating world, but with every day that passes by, I think I'm getting closer. Could you please make him tall and handsome and a good dancer? And this time around, could you let my brothers approve of him and not give him a hard time?

Was she ready for God to point someone in her direction? She believed so. It had been so long since she'd had romantic feelings for someone or even gone out on a romantic date. Being burned in the past by love wasn't a strong enough reason anymore to stay single. And after seeing how thoroughly Joshua had moved on with his own life, she was determined to follow suit.

Thanks to Jasper, her brothers, as well as Declan and Finn, had been apprised of the injunction she had filed against the Ransom brothers. They had invited her to a little celebration at the Moose Café. Although she felt a little bit guilty about celebrating Joshua's misfortune, Honor was now being hailed as a conquering hero. The niggling sensation in the pit of her stomach sure didn't feel like victory.

"Let's raise a mug of hot chocolate to Honor!" Cameron said in a triumphant voice as he raised his drink high in the air.

Everyone joined in, shouting her name and offering her congratulations. She looked around the table. Her nephew, Aidan—Liam and Ruby's son—had a whipped cream mustache that made her grin. He was sitting next to his best friend, Oliver, Finn's stepson from his marriage to Maggie Richards. Finn had recently adopted Oliver, so he was now Oliver O'Rourke. Grace was giving baby Eva a bottle as Boone sat beside her, while Liam was sitting back in his chair as Ruby rested her head against his shoulder. Even Jasper and Hazel looked peaceful and content. As much as they fussed and feuded with one another, Honor knew their love story was epic. Cameron's wife, Paige, was gently blowing on her daughter Emma's hot cocoa, making sure it wasn't too hot for the toddler.

Honor felt a sense of pride as she gazed upon the members of her family. Finn and Declan O'Rourke and their wives, Maggie and Annie, were honorary members of the Prescott brood. And Sophie was also, along with her husband, Noah Catalano. *This should be enough*, she realized. A fantastic family and great friends who showered her with love and affection. She was an auntie several times over. If she never met the man of her dreams, she would still be loved. Always.

Liam began to loudly clink his mug with a spoon. "Attention! Attention!" he called out. "Since we're all gathered here celebrating Honor's brilliant move to protect this town, Ruby and I wanted to make an announcement." There was a feeling of expectation hovering in the air. Everything stilled and hushed.

Ruby smiled at her husband, then swung her gaze around the table. "We're expecting a baby!" she announced.

A deafening roar erupted at the table. Everyone began hooting and hollering. Jasper was yelling louder than anyone. Grace made a point to cover baby Eva's ears.

Honor got up from her seat and made her way to her brother's side. She threw her arms around his neck. "Oh, Liam, I'm so happy for all of you. You must be over the moon about it."

Liam grinned, making him look even more handsome. "I'm thrilled. We've been blessed with such abundance. I didn't dare to hope for more." He shrugged. "But the good Lord saw fit to add to our family."

"He sure did," Honor said. "No two people deserve it more than you and Ruby. You're wonderful parents." After everything the couple had endured when Ruby was presumed dead in an avalanche, Honor couldn't be more overjoyed for their incredible news. It had taken them years to find their way back to one another, but their love had endured adversity.

"I can't wait till it happens for you," Liam said, squeezing her hand. "You're so supportive of everyone else's happy news."

"From your lips to God's ears," she said in a teasing voice. "I think I'm ready to move forward in that area."

"Good," Liam said. "It's about time."

Boone stood up and raised his mug. "Now, let's make a toast to Ruby and Liam. And big brother-to-be, Aidan. May your new addition be healthy and happy." Aidan was grinning from ear-to-ear.

The café was filled with joy and euphoria. It had turned into the perfect family night. A cell phone rang out amidst the chaos.

"Sorry, I'm on call at the clinic," Liam said, holding up his phone and walking away from the table.

"I can't believe I'm going to be a great-grandfather again," Jasper said, rubbing his grizzled jaw. "It seems like just yesterday I was sledding with Boone, Liam and Cameron on Cupid's Hill when they were little tykes."

"I want to go sledding!" Aidan cried out. "Can you take me, Jasper?"

Hazel shook her head. "Aidan. Jasper might break a hip if he takes you sledding." She leaned in toward him and said in a loud whisper, "He's not as young as he thinks he is."

Jasper shook a finger at Hazel. "I heard that. A person is only as old as they feel."

"So you're one hundred and five," Hazel cracked, throwing her head back in laughter. Jasper frowned at his wife, but his lips twitched with amusement.

Liam rushed back to the table, his expression tense and full of concern.

"Guys, I've got to head over to the clinic." His gaze swung toward Honor. "It seems Joshua Ransom's daughter took a bad fall. He's on his way into town with the child right now."

Honor jumped up from her seat and walked over toward Liam. Her pulse was skittering. She couldn't imagine how frantic Joshua would be under these circumstances. Violet was his entire world.

"Is it bad?" she asked.

Liam's expression was grim. "I'm not sure. I need

to head over right now. I want to be at the clinic when he arrives."

"I'm coming with you, Liam," she said.

He frowned down at her. "Are you sure that's a good idea?"

She bit her lip. "Not really, but if I was in his shoes, I'd want some company. I have no idea if I'll be welcome, but I think considering what we meant to each other in the past it feels like the right thing to do."

"Okay," he nodded. "Let's go."

She went back to her seat and grabbed her purse and coat, then quickly trailed after Liam.

"Honor!" Boone called after her. She turned around and eyed him warily. He had caught up to her. His expression radiated concern.

"Boone. I've got to go. It's an emergency."

"Why don't you just stay here with us? It's not wise to get wrapped up in Joshua's personal life," he warned. "You don't need to get pulled back in."

Why was Boone continuing to treat her like a child? It was beyond irritating. "The last time I checked I'm an adult. I'm gainfully employed and I live on my own. I'm no longer the naive teenager who had stars in her eyes. Please stop questioning my decisions!"

Boone opened his mouth to reply, but she turned on her heel and raced to catch up with Liam, who had left the café. When she walked outside, Honor spotted her brother revving up his car across the street. She raced over, then hustled into the passenger seat.

Please, Lord, she prayed. *Let Violet be all right. It will destroy Joshua if his baby girl is seriously injured. We might not be in the best place right now, but I still*

*care about what happens to Joshua. I don't want him
to be in pain.*

And therein lay her truths. She still cared. Their
love story had ended a long time ago, but it didn't mean
she had ever stopped loving him as a human being. It
was different from being *in* love with him, but it was
still powerful. The ties binding them together meant
she couldn't turn her back on him when he was in need.
And beautiful, sweet Violet had touched something inside of Honor that had been dormant for a long time.
It had frightened her to feel such intense emotions for
Joshua's daughter, but she knew exactly where they
stemmed from—the loss of the baby she and Joshua
had created.

It wasn't easy dealing with all the feelings she had
stuffed down for so many years, but Honor knew she
needed to offer support to Joshua and Violet. She
prayed Joshua wouldn't be upset by her presence at
the clinic, because there was no force on earth that
could stop her from being there.

Joshua couldn't remember a time in his life when
he had been so terrified. He had broken every speed
record in Love, Alaska, in order to get Violet to Dr.
Liam Prescott's clinic. Violet screamed the entire way.
His heart had broken listening to her cries. All he'd
wanted to do was hold her in his arms and make her
feel better. Joshua had uttered more prayers than he'd
ever imagined possible.

Because neither Theo nor Winnie had been at the
house this evening when Violet had fallen, he was all
alone in a very scary situation.

As he pulled up in front of the clinic, he immediately noticed it was ablaze with lights. He vaulted out of the truck and raced to unbuckle Violet. Her face was blotchy and red. She was whimpering and her eyes were pink from crying. Joshua cradled her as gently as he possibly could in his arms. The last thing he wanted to do was inflict more pain on her.

As soon as he walked up to the front door, it swung open. Liam stood in the entranceway, ushering him inside.

"Come on into the examining room," Liam said, leading him down the hall.

Honor was standing there with wide eyes, wringing her hands. There was a look of strain on her face. "I thought you might need a friend," she said.

Although he was still furious with her regarding the injunction, Joshua couldn't ignore the sense of relief he felt upon seeing her. Even though they were at odds over the Diamond R, Honor knew him on a level most people didn't. They had history. Somehow it made him feel better to have her here. Now he didn't feel so alone.

He nodded at her, tacitly giving her permission to come with them into the examining room. Once they were inside the room, Liam began to pepper him with questions.

"Can you tell me what happened, Joshua?" Liam asked.

Joshua had to talk over the sound of Violet's wails. Every now and again she would stop crying, only to start up again. "She fell down the basement stairs." He let out an agonized sound. "I ran down there to get something. I left her playing in the living room. I can't believe she toddled all the way over to the base-

ment door." He scratched his jaw. "I should have realized she could scoot over there in the blink of an eye."

"These things happen. You can't dwell on that part,"
Liam said in a gentle voice. "I'm going to lay her down
on her back so I can examine her. Just stand right next
to me so she stays as calm as possible."

Joshua laid Violet down on the examining table.
She held out her arms so he would pick her up. Joshua
was in agony. His daughter was too little to understand
what was going on. As Liam examined her, Joshua
spoke to her in a calm, soothing voice. He began playing peekaboo with her and trying to distract her. After
a few minutes, Liam sat Violet up.

"I'm going to do some X-rays on her left arm. Judging by the way she's holding it and her reaction to my
touching it, it could be broken. And I'd like to check on
her leg as well. She could have broken several bones in
the fall. We just have to make certain. She's not showing any signs of a concussion, but we should watch out
for them. Loss of balance. Headache. And I also want
to rule out any internal injuries."

Joshua ran a hand over his face. He felt incredibly
guilty. "I can't believe this," he muttered. "She's just
a baby."

"It's going to be all right, Joshua. Violet is in great
hands. Liam will figure out what's going on," Honor
said in a comforting tone.

"Why don't we just take her down the hall to get
the X-rays and then I'll be able to see what's going on
with her," Liam explained. "I'll give you a vest to wear,
Joshua, so you can hold Violet and not have to worry
about exposure to any radiation."

Joshua nodded, handing Violet over to Honor. She

didn't fuss or make a peep. Violet's big blue eyes were focused on Honor. Clearly, she'd won her over with her sweet, honeyed voice and warm smiles. Honor projected a caring, sensitive vibe. It was one of the many reasons Joshua had fallen for her.

Honor swayed back and forth with Violet as Liam took Joshua into the X-ray room and helped him into his vest.

"We'll be done shortly," Liam said to Honor, taking Violet from her arms and bringing her into the room with Joshua. Honor gave him an encouraging thumbs-up sign before the door was closed.

Taking the X-rays wasn't as simple as Joshua had hoped. Violet wriggled around like a fish on a hook. He let out a huge sigh of relief when Liam told him he'd managed to get a great picture of Violet's extremities.

As soon as they returned to the examination room, he began to pace back and forth. It killed him that his daughter was in so much pain. Violet had begun to softly cry again. He'd been negligent. He didn't think he could ever forgive himself for hurting Violet. Honor didn't overstep. She stood by as a support system without being overbearing.

"This is all my fault!" he said in an agonized voice as he gently held Violet in his arms. He worried about hurting her by moving her body or brushing against her.

He felt a soothing touch on his shoulder. "Don't blame yourself, Joshua. It was an accident," Honor said. "The way you feel about Violet speaks volumes. You would never hurt her intentionally."

"I should have watched her more closely. In the past few days she's been extra curious about her surroundings. I know how fast she can move when she's motivated."

"Blaming yourself is wasting a lot of energy. Why don't you focus on next steps? What can you do to make Violet feel better? Does she have a favorite treat, like Popsicles or chocolate milk? What about a blanket that makes her feel better or a favorite doll?"

"That's a great idea, Honor. Thanks." He shook his head. "I just hope she's going to be all right."

Honor sent him an encouraging smile. "I think she will be. She's not crying as much as when you first arrived. I know she's in pain, but I think she's probably scared, too. Taking a tumble is frightening."

"You're right about that." Perhaps her injuries weren't as terrible as he'd imagined on the drive to the clinic.

Dear Lord. Please grant Violet favor. She's just a baby. She doesn't even understand what's happening. Please give her comfort and healing.

"I appreciate you being here, Honor. A few hours ago I never would have imagined feeling this way, but despite what's going on with the ranch, when I saw you standing by the exam room door, I was grateful."

"It must have been terrifying for you." She made a tutting noise. "And for Violet."

"It all happened so fast. I'm still wondering how it all happened so quickly."

Suddenly, Liam reappeared in the room. "I've studied the images. The arm is fractured. But the good news is, no other broken bones. Due to her age, she'll heal quickly. There aren't signs of a concussion or anything more ominous. Please keep me in the loop if she exhibits any additional symptoms, although I'm confident she'll be on the mend soon."

"Praise the Lord," Honor cried out, clapping her hands together.

Joshua let out a ragged sigh. He pressed a kiss on Violet's cheek, overcome with relief and joy. He carefully maneuvered so as not to give her any additional pain or aggravate the injury. She nuzzled her face against his chest and stuck her thumb firmly in her mouth. He looked down at her, knowing full well he was wearing his heart on his sleeve. "What a blessing! I'm grateful for your dedication, Liam."

"That's what I'm here for, Joshua. To make things better. Now I need to put a cast on her arm." He made a face. "At her age, it isn't easy to sit still, especially when you're in pain."

Joshua looked down at Violet. She was so small and vulnerable. He couldn't wait until this night was nothing more than a memory.

"Why don't you hold her in your lap and I'll get it done as fast as I possibly can?" Liam suggested in a gentle voice. Joshua was thoroughly impressed with Dr. Liam Prescott. Six years ago he'd intensely disliked Honor's brother. He was convinced the feeling had been mutual. It was amazing how people could grow and change for the better.

Joshua sat down and held Violet in his lap. He held her free hand as Liam placed the cast on her arm. Considering everything she'd been through this evening, Violet barely fussed. Part of his heart ached at the weary expression imprinted on his daughter's face. She'd been put through the wringer. Her little body was near exhaustion.

"Why don't you take this little lady home? My work here is done. Violet looks like she's ready to crash."

Liam tousled Violet's blond curls. "I can't say I blame her. She's had quite an eventful night."

"She's been a trouper," Honor said, reaching out and brushing Violet's hair out of her eyes.

Joshua stuck out his hand to Liam, who didn't hesitate to shake it. "Thank you for responding so quickly to my call. And for everything you did for my daughter. I won't ever forget it. You can send the bill to the ranch."

"I'll do that. You're very welcome." Liam nodded. "Goodnight. I'm going to lock up the place."

Honor held the door open for Liam as he walked outside. Snow was gently falling from the inky sky. Violet turned her face upward and giggled as snowflakes landed on her face. Joshua glanced over at Honor. They met each other's gaze and smiled. Seeing Violet so full of joy was an amazing blessing.

"She's something else, isn't she?" Joshua asked.

"She sure is," Honor murmured. An emotion he couldn't pinpoint flickered in her blue-gray eyes.

He busied himself settling Violet into her car seat. Within seconds her eyes were firmly shut and she was fast asleep.

"Poor little thing," Honor said. "She needs a good night's rest."

"I won't disagree with you on that. 'Night, Honor."

"Good night, Joshua." She began to fiddle with her fingers. "I know my being here tonight doesn't change anything regarding the injunction and the Diamond R Ranch, but I'm really happy it all worked out this evening."

He felt something inside him toughen up at the mention of the injunction and Bud's ranch. When Honor had invited him and Violet to the wildlife center, he had viewed it as an olive branch being extended. A beautiful act of grace. But then she had stabbed him in the back by filing an injunction against him and Theo. When she had shown up at the clinic, it had felt so comforting and amazing. But, he had to admit, now that his fear for Violet had diminished, he was beginning to see things more clearly. It wasn't all roses and moonlight between him and Honor.

Now he had to wonder if she had a hidden agenda. Why was she bringing up the issue right now? Couldn't she let it go for one evening?

"I appreciate the fact that you came here tonight, but you're right. It doesn't change a thing. We're still on opposite sides of a very tense situation."

"I wasn't trying to make you angry," she said.

"I guess I'm beyond anger." He shook his head. "I've been racking my brain trying to reconcile the woman I used to know with the person who filed legal paperwork against me. It seemed almost spiteful." He let out a frustrated sigh. All he wanted to do was go back to the ranch and tuck Violet into bed. But he couldn't leave without getting a few things off his chest.

Honor met his gaze head-on. "It couldn't be helped. I felt you and Theo left me no choice but to explore other avenues to shut down this sale of the ranch. And I know you've had a rough night, but I'm not sorry about what I did." Sparks were practically flying from her. She seemed defiant.

"You're just prolonging the inevitable, Honor. We're Bud's heirs. Myself, Theo and Violet. I know you thought the property was being willed to the town, but that ship has sailed. Ultimately, my brother and I are going to be in control of the ranch and property. We'll decide what happens to it. Not you. And not the townsfolk!"

"I don't agree with you. An injunction is in place. That didn't happen on a lark. I think we set forth some excellent reasons why the land shouldn't be sold to a developer. We might win this."

Joshua let out a strangled sound. "We're not just going to lie down and let you run all over us. Theo flew to Anchorage the other day to meet with legal counsel." He furrowed his brow. "That injunction isn't worth the paper it's written on. I don't want to see you crushed, Honor, but you're not going to win this. You might as well resign yourself to the idea that the ranch is going to be sold."

A wounded expression passed over her face. "Tonight wasn't about legal wrangling or injunctions or Texas developers descending on this town. I actually came here this evening as a friend." She tilted her chin up. "I'm sorry that I actually thought that might be possible. Good night, Joshua."

Honor turned around and walked back toward the clinic. He opened his mouth to call out to her and apologize for his harsh words, but he reined the words back in. Joshua shouldn't feel guilty. He and Honor weren't friends. Not in the truest sense of the word.

Friends kept in touch. He hadn't seen Honor in six years. They hadn't been a part of each other's world in a very long time. She had been the great love of his life. And he didn't want or need a friend here in Love because he wasn't staying. This town had brought him nothing but pain and rejection. As soon as the lawyers were able to have the injunction withdrawn, Joshua intended to move forward with the sale of the ranch.

He was tired of allowing people to stomp all over him simply because he'd made some mistakes in the past. Who among them was perfect? When he had first arrived back in Love, Joshua had hoped the townsfolk would see he'd made something of himself. He had only been fooling himself to think they would even care. With the exception of Hazel, all the residents seemed to care about was whether or not the Ransom brothers were selling the Diamond R.

From this point forward, Joshua wasn't going to feel an ounce of guilt about selling the ranch to the Alloy Corporation. In the past few days the ranch had gotten under his skin. He had been awash in memories of a childhood and adolescence spent at the ranch. But the ranch didn't represent his future. And as he had done for the past six years, Joshua would simply stuff down the past.

He would always treasure the memories of life at the Diamond R Ranch with his family, but he had already made his peace with letting go of the property Bud had loved so much. Now if he could only relinquish his feelings for Honor.

As he drove away from the clinic he cast a glance in his rearview mirror at the back seat. He couldn't see Violet's face due to the rear-facing car seat, but he suspected she remained fast asleep. His heart swelled with love for her. Every step he took in this lifetime mattered due to his little girl. She was the reason he drew breath each and every morning. Feeling a tug in Honor's direction after all of these years was merely a distraction. He had come back to Love only for a short

period of time, to properly say goodbye to his grandfather and to help Theo settle the estate.

It was far too dangerous to get invested in this town
or in Honor Prescott.

Honor couldn't remember the last time she'd been
so incensed. Actually, she could. Six years ago when
she had discovered from Boone that Joshua had burned
the church down, Honor had been consumed with un-
bridled rage. It had seemed incomprehensible to her.
How could he have done something so horrendous?
In doing so, it had dealt their relationship a final devastating blow. All their plans for the future had been
extinguished by his dangerous actions.

And now he had treated her with such cruelty and
condescension. She didn't care what he thought! Her
presence here tonight at the clinic hadn't been motivated by anything other than concern. The moment
Liam had told her about Violet's fall, Honor had wanted
to be by his side to help him deal with the situation.
She had acted on pure instinct.

As she sat down in the passenger seat of Liam's car,
she slammed the door behind her.

"Hey! Easy on the door. What's wrong?" Liam asked
as he revved his engine. "Did something go down between you and Joshua while I was locking up?"

Honor clenched her teeth. She felt like exploding.
"I don't want to talk about it," she muttered.

"Uh-oh," Liam said. "That doesn't sound good.
Whenever Ruby utters that phrase, I head for the hills."

Honor threw her hands in the air. "Joshua had the
nerve to question my motives. He brought up the in-

junction and we got into it. I came here tonight with the best of intentions. He should be—"

"Grateful?" Liam asked, shooting her a pointed look before turning his eyes back toward the road.

"Yes, he should. Don't you think so?"

A small sigh slipped past his lips. "Honor, I think you should give Joshua a break."

She sucked in a shocked breath. "What do you mean? You can't stand Joshua. Why are you taking his side?"

"Simmer down, cowgirl. First of all, I don't dislike him. I hated what he did to the church and this town." His voice softened. "And to you. As your big brother, it gutted me to see you with a broken heart. But I let go of all those feelings a long time ago. My faith tells me to turn the other cheek. So that's what I did."

A groundswell of love for her brother rose up within her. He had always been the most tenderhearted of all her siblings.

"Can you really expect Joshua to be focused on gratitude when you filed the injunction against him?"

Tears welled in Honor's eyes. "It wasn't personal."

Liam pulled up in front of the Moose Café and put his car in Park. He turned toward her, wiping away a stray tear on her cheek with his thumb. "I'm not criticizing you. I think it was a brilliant move designed to protect this town. I admire you more than mere words can express. You showed pluck and grit and ingenuity."

Honor's lips quivered. "Why can't Joshua see it that way? He made it seem as if I'm being malicious."

"Sis, you don't have a mean bone in your body. If Joshua blew up at you tonight, I would say he's simply hurting and frustrated. He looked scared tonight. Really petrified. He's under a lot of strain on the heels of Bud's passing. And he was terrified for Violet."

Suddenly, she felt ashamed of herself. Liam was right. Joshua was in mourning for his grandfather. Maybe it had been wrong of her to file the injunction when he was at a low moment. She bit her lip. "I know. I can't imagine how terrifying it must have been for both of them."

"I know what it feels like to be a single father," he said. "It can be really lonely and you question whether or not you're doing a decent job as a parent. I empathize with him. That being said, why do you care so much? Isn't he leaving soon to go back home?"

Honor knit her brows together. Liam's question threw her for a loop. "What? I—I don't really care all that much. It's just that I'm trying to be cordial with him. Isn't that turning the other cheek? I've tried to move beyond what happened between us in the past. As painful as it was for me to go through all of it with him, I realize he's grown and changed. He's been married. He's a father now to a beautiful little girl. I've moved on."

She met Liam's gaze. "Have you, Honor? Really and truly? Because from where I'm sitting, it doesn't seem like it. The look on your face when I told you about Violet's accident was very telling."

Honor rolled her eyes. "I'm not in love with him anymore if that's what you're insinuating. Those feelings died a long time ago."

"I'm not saying you're still in love with him. But what I am saying is that if you're not careful, you're going to fall in love all over again with your ex-fiancé."

Chapter Eight

❧

Joshua stood in the stables saddling up Blaze for a ride across the property. He felt excitement bubbling up inside him at the prospect of being at one with the Alaskan landscape. Since he'd been back home, riding had become one of his favorite pastimes. There was really nothing like it. It filled something inside his soul like nothing else could.

There had been a small snow squall late last night, but it had barely added to the accumulation already on the ground. Love, Alaska, was a wintry wonderland. He couldn't deny how much he enjoyed being back at the ranch. It brought back to life a part of him he thought he'd buried a long time ago. It was hard to imagine not ever being able to ride across this landscape again.

Theo was on Violet duty while Joshua was taking this opportunity to venture out on the property. His brother had felt awful about not being around when the accident took place. As a treat, Uncle Theo had brought a huge teddy bear for Violet from a local gift shop called Keepsakes. Violet had embraced the stuffed animal with open arms, smothering it with hugs and endless kisses. She had gifted Theo with a million-dollar smile in return for his kindness. He shook his head at the irony in Theo purchasing the toy at the same store that he'd broken into on a dare back in his rebellious years.

Joshua couldn't wait to have some alone time out on the range. He needed to clear his head regarding last night. Had he been too harsh on Honor? Or had he been right on point? He had no way of knowing since, when it came to Honor, he always seemed to lose his objectivity.

Last night when he had returned to the ranch, he'd gotten down on his knees and prayed about the situation. He was now a man who didn't like volatile situations or drama. It reminded him all too much of things he would rather forget.

"Mr. Ransom. Can I have a few minutes?"

Joshua swung his gaze up. Cal Abilene, the ranch foreman, was standing in front of him with a look of concern carved on his face. He had his cowboy hat in his hand and his eyes swirled with strong emotions.

"Sure thing, Cal. What's up?" he asked. From everything he had heard from Bud, as well as what he had seen with his own eyes, Cal was a great ranch foreman. Hardworking and honest, Cal had been at the Diamond R for almost twenty years. The ranch's success was directly related to Cal's strong work ethic.

Cal raked a hand through his shoulder-length dark hair.

"Would you mind telling me if you're going to be selling the place? If so, I need to start looking for a new position here in town or head to the Kenai Peninsula where there are more opportunities to work on a ranch."

Joshua felt his heart sink. How could he and Theo have been so thoughtless? The Diamond R had employees who counted on their paychecks to stay afloat. Selling the ranch would have a trickle-down effect.

"Honestly, Cal, things are up in the air at the moment. I'm sure you heard about the injunction filed against us?"

Cal nodded. "I sure did. Honor has a lot more pluck than I ever gave her credit for," Cal said with a light chuckle.

"I'll be straight with you. As soon as the injunction is lifted, Theo and I plan to accept an offer for the ranch. To be honest, I'm not sure if the outfit buying the Diamond R will keep you and the others on. That hasn't been discussed."

Cal's face fell. "I'd like you to know the people who work on this ranch have been here for years. We work hard. We've always been invested in this place." He twisted his mouth. "It's hard to imagine this ranch changing hands. Bud poured his heart and soul into the Diamond R."

Joshua felt a prickle of guilt. "I know he did. And if it's okay by you, I'll make sure to inquire as to whether the Alloy Corporation will be in need of a foreman and ranch hands."

Cal scoffed. "For the dude ranch? No, thanks, Mr. Ransom. That doesn't interest me. But I appreciate your giving it to me straight about selling the ranch. Now at least I know what I need to do." With a nod of his head, Cal strode away from the stables.

Joshua stood by Blaze and watched as Cal quickly

disappeared from sight. He felt awful. He had been so consumed by his own agenda and concern for Violet's future that he hadn't considered the people whose lives would be drastically altered if the Diamond R was sold.

Cal had driven the point home. Many lives were going to be affected by the sale of the ranch. Not just the townsfolk of Love, but the dedicated employees who had worked at the Diamond R for years. They would all have to seek employment elsewhere, or even leave Love in order to make a living. It wasn't fair to them, but there was nothing he could do to change things. He had already agreed to sell. His future was in Seattle.

As he mounted Blaze and headed out across the property, Joshua let go of all the things that were burdening him. He took a deep breath of the fresh Alaskan air and began to gallop away from the ranch. Craggy mountains stretched out before him in the distance. There was nothing but wide-open spaces in front of him. He turned his face up toward the sky and allowed the sun's rays to wash over him. He flew like the wind on Blaze's back, feeling unfettered for the first time in ages.

From a distance, he spotted a person on horseback galloping toward him. As soon as the rider drew closer, Joshua recognized Honor seated on Lola. He had forgotten how close he was to the property line for the wildlife center.

"Honor," he said, tipping his cowboy hat in her direction by way of greeting.

She reined in her horse, bringing Lola to a stop not far from him. "Hi, Joshua. I was just heading toward the Diamond R so I could check on the newborn calves."

The calves. He had almost forgotten all about them. "It's nice of you to take time out from the wildlife center to check on them."

"Bud trusted me to do it a few times a week. He and I stayed close over the years. I wouldn't feel right about stopping until a decision is made about the ranch."

"I'm headed in that direction. We can ride together." He frowned. "Unless you'd rather not."

"I think the great outdoors is big enough for both of us," she cracked, making a none-too-subtle reference to their war of words the other night.

"You're right about that. It's beautiful out here. Majestic. Seattle is a nice place to live, but it's not this," he said, scanning the area around them. This Alaskan vista was one of the most spectacular sights he had ever seen.

"How's Violet this morning? If I may ask?"

"Of course you can. She's doing well. Theo is probably spoiling her as we speak."

"It's all right to do so now and again. After all, she went through the wringer due to her accident. And she wasn't the only one. I saw the alarm on your face. The love you feel for Violet is palpable."

"Once you become a mother you'll see how it is," he said. "You always worry."

Honor visibly winced. "I can imagine," she murmured.

"I remember riding out here with you a lot," Joshua said, meeting Honor's gaze. Were the memories as indelible for her as they were for him? He could picture in his mind's eye her long chestnut-colored hair whipping in the breeze and the look of joy on her face.

A slight smile twitched at her lips. "I remember the time we were looking for a herd of wild mustangs."

Joshua laughed. "Bud told me if I caught one of 'em, I could keep him."

Honor made a face. "Little did we know it was easier said than done."

His grandfather had been a mischievous person. It had tickled him to no end to play jokes on him and Theo. On this occasion Bud had convinced Joshua to go out looking for wild mustangs. He'd fallen for it hook, line and sinker, not realizing that catching one was a near impossible task. In the end, he had come up empty-handed.

"I miss him," he said, blurting out the sentiment that had been sitting on his heart ever since he'd learned of his grandfather's death.

"Me too. He was truly one-of-a-kind. Sort of like Jasper."

Joshua wrinkled his nose. "I'm not sure anyone on earth is quite like Jasper."

They both laughed. God had broken the mold when He had created Mayor Jasper Prescott and everybody knew it.

"I will say he's done something amazing with Operation Love. At the end of the day, people want to find love and a soft place to fall," Honor said. "That's happening here in town now thanks to my grandfather."

A soft place to fall. That's exactly what he'd wanted to give Honor all those years ago. And he knew she would have given it back in return. He wasn't sure he would ever fully get over it. But he hoped life would bring him a loving partner and a mother for Violet. Everyone needed someone to lean on, to pray with, to grow old beside them. Perhaps one of these days God would hear his most fervent prayer.

"What about you?" he asked, blurting out the question he'd been dying to ask. "Are you signed up for the program?"

Honor looked at him, startled. "No, I'm not, but I appreciate what Jasper is doing for this town. Lately I've begun to realize that we all need that special someone in our lives. Who doesn't want the fairy tale?" Her voice sounded soft and vulnerable. It made him want to sweep her into his arms and hold on to her for as long as she would allow.

"It sounds like you're right where you need to be. There are lots of Alaskan bachelors in this town." Joshua tried to stifle a sudden spurt of jealousy. He wanted Honor to be happy, but the thought of her settling down with another man bothered him. He couldn't shake the feeling off or stop the images racing through his mind of Honor walking down the aisle and cradling a newborn in her arms.

Still, after all of this time, Joshua felt cheated out of the life he had envisioned leading with Honor.

Silence descended upon them as they neared the Diamond R. For a moment something hung in the air between them. Neither one mentioned the tension of the other night, but it hung between them like a live grenade. He didn't know whether to broach the subject or simply leave it alone.

"Well, I should go see to the calves," Honor said. "I'm glad Violet is feeling better. You must be relieved."

"Thanks. I'm a happy man," he said, his apology getting swallowed up by his pride. He stood by everything he'd said to her, but his timing and delivery was questionable. Joshua should never have barked at her when she'd showed up at the clinic simply to offer support. It had been less than gracious.

And be kind to one another, tenderhearted, forgiving one another even as God for Christ's sake hath forgiven you. The Bible verse from *Ephesians* ran through his mind, serving as an admonishment for the harsh way he had treated Honor. Despite the fact that she had filed the injunction, Joshua needed to forgive her. Hadn't he wanted the townsfolk to offer him the same grace?

Joshua watched Honor dismount from Lola and head toward the barn. He felt a knot in his stomach as his gaze trailed after her. Why did it always seem as if Honor was leaving him? Pretty soon he would be leaving Love, never to return. The ramifications of it sat heavily on his chest. The thought of never seeing Honor again made him ache inside. Despite the anger he felt toward her for filing the injunction, Joshua couldn't forget what they'd meant to each other in the past.

Joshua led Blaze toward the stables and placed him in his stall. The horse was working his mouth, letting Joshua know he'd enjoyed their ride across the property. After cleaning his tack and picking out his hooves, he treated the horse to an apple. As Joshua headed toward the house, he felt as if he was coming home. *Home.* He had never quite felt that way about Seattle. He'd always believed it was because he hadn't yet bought a house to live in, but he now realized it wasn't true. Home was a feeling. It settled inside you like a warm, comfy blanket.

Seattle didn't have this stunning vista. He couldn't ride to his heart's delight at a moment's notice. He didn't have history there. Seattle was a blank slate. He had always considered that a good thing, but now that he was back in his hometown, he was beginning to think it might not be.

Joshua could honestly picture himself settling down here with Violet. Living at the ranch would be a dream come true. The thought served as a jolt to the system. Where had it come from? He wasn't sticking around Love any longer than was absolutely necessary. It was silly of him to imagine a life that could never be possible. He needed to be realistic and focus on moving forward with his life, not only for his sake, but for Violet's as well.

While she checked on Bud's calves at the ranch, Honor tried to keep her thoughts from straying toward Joshua. Seeing him enjoying a ride on Blaze had been a little surprising. It really shouldn't have been, considering how much he had always loved horses, but she'd convinced herself that Joshua had changed over the years from the young man she'd known.

She had been wrong. The adult version of Joshua clearly still enjoyed riding. A warm feeling settled over her at the realization that he was still the same person she had loved so dearly. Seeing him seated on Blaze took her back to all of the adventures they had enjoyed on Bud's property. The Diamond R Ranch had been their stomping grounds. Those carefree moments were permanently seared on Honor's heartstrings.

"You like all this undivided attention, don't you?" Honor asked as she gently patted one of the calves. She wasn't sure if it was her imagination, but the calf seemed to be smiling at her. There were five calves in all who had been born in the last few weeks. Two had been born early, but all five of them were in good condition.

"Can you blame him?" The rich tone of Joshua's voice startled her. She swung her gaze up to meet his. He was standing a few feet away with his arms folded across his chest. He was leaning against a wooden beam. She had no idea how long he'd been standing there.

"I don't mean to interrupt. I was sitting up at the main house and feeling curious about the calves. Violet is napping, so I figured I'd pop my head in. Winnie is keeping an eye on her."

"It's fine. They're your calves, after all," she said. "I'm pleased to report they're all in fine condition."

Joshua nodded. "That's in large part due to you, Honor."

Honor grinned. Bud had called her over to the ranch when each of the calves had been born. The memory was a sweet one. "Bud had me wrapped around his little finger. This ranch was his whole world. He cared about every aspect of it."

For a moment they locked gazes. Her words hung in the air, serving as a reminder of the huge divide between them regarding the Diamond R.

Her cell phone began buzzing insistently, shattering the silence. She took her phone out and glanced at the caller ID. It was a call from the wildlife center. "Sorry. I have to take this call."

"No problem," he murmured. "Take your time."

The voice of Priscilla Walters, one of her employees, rang in her ear as soon as she said hello.

"Honor! I've been looking everywhere for you."

"Hey, Priscilla. I'm at the Diamond R checking on Bud's calves. I let Clay know before I headed over here so there would be coverage at the center." There was an urgency to Priscilla's voice that was unsettling.

"Clay is out checking the fences," Priscilla quickly explained. "He forgot to mention you'd headed over to the ranch."

There had recently been an issue when one of the animals had managed to slip through a gap in the fence. She had spent the better part of a day out in the van trying to locate the heifer. They were now regularly making the rounds to ensure no more animals got loose.

"What's going on?" Honor asked. "Is something wrong?"

"We just got a call from Gunther. He spotted a small arctic fox over by Nottingham Woods not too far from the entrance. Gunther said it's been there since yesterday and it may be hurt or abandoned since it hasn't moved. He's not sure how old it is."

Honor made a clucking sound. "Gunther probably thought the mama fox was nearby at first, but if it's still by itself something may have happened to the mother. She may not be alive or she's rejected the baby fox for some reason."

"Can you ride out there?" Priscilla asked. "There's a few preschool kids who are coming for a tour today so I'd like to stay put. And I can't reach Clay. There's probably no service where he is."

"Sure thing," Honor said, not wanting to leave the children in the lurch.

Although she hated to miss the visit by the small group of children, locating the arctic fox and making sure it was safe and sound was important. A young fox who was on its own and possibly injured was a pressing matter.

"I'll head right over there and check it out," Honor said.

When she hung up, Joshua shot her a questioning look.

"There's an arctic fox out in the wild. It might be hurt or abandoned. We're not sure how old it is. I need to head out to Nottingham Woods to check on it," she explained.

Joshua's eyes widened. "How are you going to do that without a vehicle?"

Honor sighed. She had completely forgotten that she'd ridden Lola over to the Diamond R. It would take her forever to ride all the way to the Nottingham Woods on her horse. And if the arctic fox needed medical attention, Honor wouldn't be able to transport it to the wildlife center.

"I'd be happy to drive you over there," Joshua offered. "It's been a while since I've been to Nottingham Woods."

Honor shook her head. "I couldn't ask you to do that."

"You're not asking me. I'm offering," he said in a firm voice. "I can also have one of the ranch hands bring Lola back to the wildlife center for you."

"Thank you, Joshua," Honor said. "I accept. Do

you mind if we leave right now?" she asked, anxious to find the fox.

Joshua laughed. "No problem. I just need to let Winnie know I'm going to be out for a while so she can watch Violet. I'll be right back," he said, beating a fast path out of the barn and heading toward the main house.

After grabbing her belongings, Honor walked toward Bud's truck. She only had to wait a few moments before Joshua came back outside and met her by the vehicle. He opened the door for her and she stepped up into the truck. Joshua got behind the wheel and headed off toward Nottingham Woods. It was roughly a fifteen-minute drive from the ranch. As Joshua drove, they passed moose crossing signs and a desolate patch of road with nothing more than snow-covered trees decorating the landscape. The view of the mountains became even more magnificent the closer they drove toward the woods.

As they approached Nottingham Woods, Honor made a mental note to come back up here soon to do some hiking. As a kid, Jasper had taken her and her brothers spelunking in one of the nearby caves. As a teenager, Honor had brought Joshua to the caves. In a wildly romantic gesture, Joshua had carved their initials in the stone wall. *J.R. loves H.P. forever.* To this day, no man had ever made Honor feel the way Joshua had in that moment. Adored. Treasured. Well loved.

Once they arrived, a large cedar sign welcomed them to Nottingham Woods. Joshua turned the truck into the entrance and put it in Park. Honor opened her door and stepped down. She immediately began scouring the area. She knew from experience that arctic foxes could easily blend into the scenery due to their white coats. Honor began walking toward the trail and searching the area for any trace of the animal. Joshua walked a few feet behind her. It was nice to have another set of eyes and ears.

Frustration and worry set in after a half hour. Trying to look on the bright side, Honor reckoned the fox could have been reunited with its mother or found its way back to the den.

All of a sudden, a slight sound caused her to stop in her tracks. "Did you hear that?" she asked Joshua. He nodded instead of speaking. Clearly, he was trying not to spook any animals.

She turned her head to a patch of trees twenty feet away from the trail. As she moved closer, the sounds became more distinct. Honor picked up her pace. She gasped as she came face-to-face with a pure white arctic fox. It was curled up and emitting whimpering sounds. Although it wasn't a baby, it appeared to be under a year old.

Honor saw its weakened condition and the signs that the fox hadn't been eating. It was clear to her that the fox had been injured, which explained why it appeared malnourished. It hadn't been able to forage for food. It meant Honor needed to transport it back to the center. Getting the arctic fox proper nourishment and shelter was crucial for its long-term survival.

She reached out and touched the fox. It was shaking like a leaf. "I'm not going to hurt you, sweet pea." Honor tried to make her voice reassuring and tender. With the utmost gentleness, she lifted it up on its legs. Joshua knelt beside her, allowing her to take the lead but staying close for support. Almost immediately, the fox collapsed. Honor could see there was something going on with its legs.

"She can't walk on her own," she said to Joshua. "I'm going to take her to the center for rehabilitation."

"Why don't you head to the truck and open up the back for me? I'll carry her," Joshua said.

She watched as Joshua reached out and scooped the small fox up into his arms. Honor took off at a fast clip and began walking toward the vehicle. She flung open the back door of the truck, not wanting to waste a moment in getting the animal inside.

After the harsh words they had exchanged, Joshua would have been the last person she would ever want to help her out. At this moment, she wouldn't want to be with anyone else but him.

Chapter Nine

Honor stood by the truck and watched as Joshua gingerly held the arctic fox in his arms. She couldn't help but admire Joshua as he strode toward her, his steps full of power and purpose. A sigh slipped past her lips. He was dressed in a nice-fitting pair of blue jeans and a hunter green parka. A cowboy hat sat perched on his head. There was no debating he was much better-looking than all of the single men in this town put together. A true Alaskan hottie! Her cheeks felt heated at the admission.

He placed the arctic fox in the back of the truck on top of one of her blankets, then firmly closed the door. Honor quickly situated herself in the passenger seat. Joshua sat in the driver's seat and cast a glance behind him at the fox. He reached to turn on the radio, his arm brushing against hers in the process, causing an electric pulse to run through her. Being so close to Joshua was doing a number on her. There was an awareness that always flared between them whenever they were in close proximity. At the same time, Honor felt comfortable in his strong, steady presence. Their shared history bonded them for life.

He revved the engine and began to drive away from Nottingham Woods.

"Thanks for bringing me out here, Joshua. You've been a big help," Honor said, gratitude welling up inside her.

"Hanging out with you twice in one day is pretty suspicious. I'm beginning to think you're following me," he said in a teasing voice.

Honor rolled her eyes. She snapped her fingers. "You figured me out. And here I was trying to be subtle."

"Isn't that how we started dating? You used to trail after me all the time until I noticed you."

"You wish, Ransom," she said, shaking her head.

His low chuckle sounded like it radiated from deep inside him. They both knew the true story. Joshua had been the one to chase Honor. He had worn down her initial defenses with his tenderness and boyish charm. She had been defenseless to resist him.

"So what's your theory on the fox? Was she abandoned?" Joshua asked.

Honor nodded. "No, I don't think so. She's not a baby. I would say she's about nine months old or so. Arctic foxes are on their own from a fairly young age and are forced to fend for themselves. Judging by her weakened state, she's malnourished. She really needs some TLC."

"Sounds like she's in good hands," Joshua said.

"The wildlife center is the perfect place for her. I'm feeling very blessed that we were able to find her in the woods."

Joshua winked at her. "Haven't you heard? There are no accidents in life. Everything happens for a reason."

No accidents in life? Honor agreed with the sentiment. Everything had a divine purpose. She had been scratching her head trying to figure out why God had placed Joshua back in Love. Surely it wasn't so he could sell Bud's ranch to the Alloy Corporation? There had to be some other reason, she reckoned. Her faith told her so.

"Well, I'm glad there's a happy ending for Bashful." The helpless look on the arctic fox's face tugged at Honor's heart.

"Bashful?" he asked with a raised eyebrow. "Like one of the seven dwarfs?"

Honor nodded. "It's the perfect name for her." She chuckled at the skeptical expression on Joshua's face. "I'm serious. She has that shy look on her face and those big ears."

"Now that you mention it, she does look a little on the bashful side," Joshua noted.

"See! I told you!" Honor said, her tone laced with triumph.

He turned toward her. "So what will happen to her?"

"First, we'll get her up to speed nutrition-wise. Then we'll rehabilitate her. She can't stand on her legs. She's been injured in some way. I'll call the vet out so he can come on over and check on her. Then we'll go from there." She found herself smiling. Although she hated the sad circumstances that led animals to the wildlife center, Honor enjoyed being the one who helped bring them to a place of healing. It was truly her calling in life.

"You really love what you do, don't you?" he asked.

"I really do. I'm so blessed. From the moment I start work in the morning until I clock out, I'm filled with such joy. Being an advocate for these animals is a huge responsibility, but it's one I completely embrace."

Joshua quirked his mouth. She could tell he was thinking about something. He was listening to every word she was saying with such rapt attention.

"What about you?" she asked, curious about his business. Bud had told her a little bit about Joshua's company. His grandfather had been extremely proud of his grandson's success, although he had always seemed wary to share information with her. Perhaps Bud had believed it would reopen old wounds. He certainly had never breathed a word to her about Violet.

"I like working in home construction and flipping houses, but I can't say I'm passionate about it. To be honest, I never really thought about it before." He frowned. "You're one of the rare ones, Honor. Most people work jobs. You have a vocation. You're living the dream."

Joshua's words made Honor's chest swell with pride. Following her passion hadn't always been easy, but she had forged through and completed her education. With her family and the Lord by her side, Honor had persevered. Boone had always advised her to keep her eyes on the prize. And she hadn't lost sight of the big dream—creating a wildlife center in Love.

As Joshua turned into the entrance to the wildlife center, Honor took a moment to survey the property. It wasn't as big as the Diamond R Ranch by any means, but it was spectacular in her opinion. She didn't want to dwell on the fact that Bud had mentioned merging the properties. It was all water under the bridge. There wasn't a single thing she could do to change it. Filing the injunction had only been about preventing the Ransom brothers from selling to a developer. If the wildlife center never gained another acre, Honor would still be content.

"Seems like you've got company," Joshua said as he pulled up to the house.

A car sat parked outside the main building. Its motor was still running.

Honor would recognize the distinctive vehicle anywhere.

"It's Lee," Honor said. Her heart sank. The timing of the attorney's visit couldn't have been worse. Joshua knew full well that Lee had helped her pursue the injunction against him and Theo.

The mood in the truck immediately became tense. She and Joshua had been getting along so well, with little or no discord. She'd thought they had turned a corner. The appearance of Lee served as a reminder that sides had been taken in the matter of Joshua's inheritance. It was as if there was a huge neon blinking sign up ahead reminding Joshua of the injunction.

Honor couldn't help but notice the change in Joshua's demeanor. His jaw was tightly clenched. He was gripping the steering wheel so hard she could see his veins threatening to burst through the skin.

Perhaps there was still some way of salvaging their goodwill toward one another.

"Would you like to stay for a bit and see how Bashful gets acclimated?" Honor asked.

"No, thanks," he said tersely. He nodded in Lee's

direction. "It looks like Lee wants your time and attention."

"Joshua, I don't want—"

His expression softened. "You don't need to say anything. We're just on opposite sides of things. That's just the way it is." He shrugged. "Maybe it's always been this way."

"What do you mean?" she asked.

"Think about it. When we first fell in love, your family tried to put up roadblocks at every turn. Then I created a bunch of them myself. Theo always had a problem with you. There was always one thing or another separating us. We never had a shot, did we?"

"That's not true!" she said. "I can't believe you've become so cynical."

"Do you blame me?" he asked in an anger-filled voice.

"Yes, I do," she said. "I guess you've forgotten what we shared, Joshua. Because it was real. It mattered. And you can try to reduce it to something trivial if you want, but it wasn't. It was pretty epic."

Their gazes locked. Honor reached out and swept her palm across Joshua's cheek. "I'm sorry if my filing the injunction hurt you. Or if you feel I've tied your hands. I truly am. But it's separate and apart from what we once meant to each other. Our love was real. And after everything I went through, I'm not going to let you say otherwise." Honor wrenched open the door and hopped out of the truck. She might have slammed the door behind her if Bashful wasn't resting peacefully. She moved toward the back of the truck and tugged the blanket toward her, bringing Bashful along with it. Next thing she knew, Joshua was beside her, lifting up the arctic fox.

"Where do you want her?" Joshua asked, looking around him.

"I can take her," Honor said, reaching out her arms for the animal. Joshua tenderly placed Bashful in her arms, then nodded at her, murmuring a quick goodbye. Lee raised his hand in greeting as soon as he spotted her. He knit his brows together as his gaze veered toward Joshua. Honor saw the questions lurking in her friend's eyes, but she had no intention of addressing them. At the moment, she was all talked out.

As Joshua roared away from the wildlife center, Honor found herself wondering how things had ever gotten so complicated between them. It seemed that they were destined to be at odds over every little thing in this world.

It had been several days since Joshua had assisted Honor with locating the wounded arctic fox at Nottingham Woods. He and Theo were making great progress on tidying up Bud's estate, with the glaring exception of the ranch. According to their lawyers, they had immediately filed all the necessary paperwork to dispute the injunction. They appeared to be very optimistic about the injunction being lifted based on similar, precedent-setting cases. The judge could render a decision any day now.

Violet seemed to be as happy as a clam despite her broken arm. Joshua was blown away by her resilience. He loved taking her out to the paddock every day so she could greet the horses with her natural brand of enthusiasm. He had even taken her to church for Sunday service. His elementary school teacher, Mrs. Henrie, had made a beeline to him after the service. It had been a nice interaction, with Joshua introducing her to Violet and Mrs. Henrie telling him how proud she was about his turning his life around. It had left Joshua feeling a tad emotional. There were still some folks in this town who thought he was worth something after all.

"I'm going a little stir-crazy," Theo announced with a loud moan as he walked into the great room and flopped onto the love seat. Violet, who was playing in her playpen while Joshua worked on the computer, stood up and held on to the sides with her hands. She gurgled at Theo. He covered his face with hands and said, "Peekaboo," causing Violet to cackle with glee. It amazed Joshua how easy it was to entertain kids. All they needed were simple things to keep them laughing and joyful.

"What does that mean? Do you want to fly the coop?" Joshua asked. He should have known Theo was bored. It had always been difficult to keep him focused.

"Yes. Don't you? This place has gotten old really quickly."

Joshua shrugged. "Not really. I like being here at the ranch. It's peaceful. And I get to ride whenever I want. Despite her broken arm, Violet seems really content. To be honest, I can't wait to teach Violet to ride when she gets old enough."

Theo snorted. "You always did love this place more than I did. That's one of the reasons I joined the army at such a young age. I wanted to spread my wings. You're like Bud. He lived and breathed this place."

"I would have been completely happy to stay and

grow old here," Joshua said in a voice clogged with emotion. Since he'd been back, Joshua had been opening himself up to the things he had buried inside him a long time ago. His hopes and dreams. His emotions. The love he'd felt for Honor. Even though he hadn't let her know it, her words had chipped away at him. She had made him feel ashamed of doubting their past relationship. Even though it hadn't resulted in a happily-ever-after, it had been the real deal.

Theo furrowed his brow. He was staring at Joshua with an intensity Joshua couldn't ignore. "Grow old? With who? Honor?"

He nodded. "That's what I wanted more than anything. We all know that didn't exactly go according to plan," Joshua said in a curt voice. What was the point in discussing Honor with Theo? He'd never been a big believer in their love story. Bringing it up would only dredge up painful memories Joshua might not be able to handle. As it was, he felt as if he was dealing with a groundswell of memories crashing over him in unrelenting waves.

"There's no reason we should have to hole up here at the ranch. We haven't done anything wrong."

Joshua made a face at his brother, then raised his eyebrows. "That's debatable."

"Well, beside the fire, but that was six years ago."

"I can think of a few things I did back when I was a teenager."

"Surely there's a statute of limitations on youthful indiscretions?" Theo asked. "God forgave me a long time ago. No one has the right to judge us. 'Judge not, lest ye be judged.'"

Joshua had to chuckle. Theo hadn't seen the inside

of a church in many years, with the exception of Bud's service. As far as Joshua could tell, his relationship with God was shaky at best. And now he was quoting from the Bible.

"Theo, I know something in the universe has shifted when you're quoting the Bible."

"You're not the only one who can change, Joshua." For once Theo wasn't making a joke. A serious expression was carved on his face.

"That's good to hear," he said with a nod. "Throughout all of the dark times in my life, I always knew the Lord was with me. That's my prayer for you as well."

Joshua reached out and clasped his brother's hand. He and Theo had always shared a tight relationship, although time and geographical distance had chipped away at it a little bit. Joshua knew he was no doubt harboring some pent-up feelings regarding the fire and taking responsibility for it. Ultimately, he'd made the decision to do so all on his own. Theo hadn't forced his hand. But he wished Theo had acted like a big brother and shielded him from the fallout.

"What do you say we head into town for Hazel's birthday celebration? It's supposed to be a big town event according to a few of my friends."

Joshua shook his head. "No, thanks. I'm not in the mood to deal with the Prescotts."

"Come on, Joshua. Hazel invited us. She wants us to be there," Theo said. He stood up and went over to the side table, then rummaged through some mail. He held up a brightly colored envelope. "Here it is. Hazel's Ageless Birthday Party. Don't you remember I mentioned it the other day?"

Joshua chuckled at the ageless theme. Leave it to Hazel to put a novel twist on celebrating a milestone year.

"Sorry. I forgot all about it. Where is it being held?" Joshua asked.

"At the Moose Café," Theo said.

He let out a groan. "Are you serious?"

"Of course I am. Hazel has been good to us. I for one want to go to the party and wish her a happy birthday. What are you afraid of? Running into the townsfolk?"

Theo's question prickled his pride. He didn't want it to seem as if he was running from the residents of Love. He wasn't a coward by any means.

"I'm not afraid of anything or anyone in this town. They've already done the worst they can do to me. And frankly, I'm a little bit over it." He inhaled deeply. "Why shouldn't we go? An invite from the birthday girl herself means something."

"That's great. I picked up a little present and a birthday card for Hazel just in case we were going to attend."

Joshua scooped up Violet from the playpen and said a little prayer about attending the celebration. If he ever wanted folks in this town to treat him with an ounce of respect, perhaps he needed to show them who he was rather than hiding away at the ranch like a hermit. Time had changed him for the better. He was a father and a businessman now. Surely they could see he had worked hard to earn redemption.

Maybe, just maybe, they would decide to show him a measure of grace.

Chapter Ten

Honor placed her gift for Hazel on the oval table laden with gaily wrapped presents. Hazel had told everyone not to buy her any gifts, but clearly, no one had listened. Knowing Hazel, Honor wouldn't be surprised one bit if she donated her gifts to a charitable organization.

"Sorry if this sounds gossipy, but isn't that your ex-fiancé who just walked in?" Her sister-in-law's blue eyes were twinkling with interest. As a journalist, Grace was always interested in people, places and things. More times than not, she couldn't keep her curiosity in check.

Honor turned her head toward the entrance. Joshua had just walked in with Theo. He was holding Violet in a baby carrier. She dragged her gaze away from the sight of him.

"That's him," she said in a cool voice to Grace.

"I saw him at the memorial for Bud. Quite a memorable face," Grace said, her lips tilted upward into a smile.

"He was always handsome," Ruby added. "It used to get him out of a lot of scrapes when he was younger."

"Not enough though," Honor said, remembering all of Joshua's brushes with the law.

"He has a kind vibe," Grace noted. "And that baby is adorable."

"I'm surprised they showed up here, although Hazel has made it quite clear she's crazy about those Ransom brothers," Ruby added.

"Let's not stare at him," Honor said, feeling a bit flushed. "He'll think we're talking about him."

"But we are," Ruby teased, her brown eyes full of mischief.

Honor watched with interest as the Ransom brothers navigated their way around the party. Honor would have guessed that Joshua would rather eat glass than show up at a birthday celebration at her brother's establishment. Perhaps Hazel herself had been the inducement. There wasn't a single soul in town who didn't adore Hazel. And she had helped Theo and Joshua host Bud's reception. Clearly, she was a fan.

She caught his eye from across the café. He waved in her direction. She nodded back. In his dark shirt and a nice-fitting pair of faded jeans, he made an eye-catching figure. Her palms began to moisten. Honor reminded herself to breathe deeply in and out. Inhale. Exhale. Why did the sight of Joshua rattle her so badly?

"I—I should go check on the cake," she muttered before turning on her heel and heading toward the kitchen. She let out a deep breath as soon as she was away from the main area of the café.

It was fairly pathetic that she was hiding out in the kitchen rather than socializing with everyone. Leave it to Hazel to have invited the Ransom brothers to her birthday party. Her kindness was legendary, and she'd always harbored a soft spot for Joshua. Back in the day it had been sort of sweet. Now it was an annoyance.

"Everything okay in here?" Hazel barked as she entered the kitchen.

Honor turned her back to Hazel as she pretended to wash her hands. Without turning around, she answered, "I'm fine. Just washing up."

"I was worried about you. You disappeared as soon as Joshua arrived. I can't help but think you're running away from something. Old feelings, perhaps?"

Honor turned around and faced Hazel. "It's just a coincidence, Hazel. You're being a bit fanciful, don't you think?"

"Believe it or not, I know a little something about love," Hazel said. "After all, I pined after Jasper for years when he barely knew I was alive."

"That's your story, not mine. I'm not pining for Joshua," she protested. "He's an ex. We're trying to be civil with one another considering we're at odds regarding the Diamond R. There's nothing more going on between us."

"Maybe not, but ever since Joshua's come back, there's been something different about you. It's as if you're lit up from the inside. You radiate a certain type of energy now that wasn't there before." She squinted at Honor. "Reminds me of how you looked when you first fell in love with Joshua. Your cheeks were always pink and you had stars in your eyes." Hazel leaned in and peered into her eyes. She nodded and let out a sound of satisfaction.

"Yep. I knew it," she said, clapping her hands together.

Honor shook her head, words of denial dancing on her tongue. What was Hazel talking about? She was being absolutely ridiculous.

"Hazel!" she said in a sharp voice. "Just because it's your birthday doesn't mean you can just spout such nonsense."

Hazel looked at her knowingly. "You don't need to say another word. Some things are as plain as the nose on your face."

There was no point in arguing with Hazel. She always liked to get the last word on any given subject. And her middle name was *matchmaker*. According to Hazel, she had paired up more people in town than Operation Love.

"I'm going back to the party," Honor said. "You should, too. After all, it isn't every day you turn… thirty-five."

Hazel burst out laughing. "Bless you, Honor. A girl after my own heart. I'll catch up to you later on."

As soon as Honor walked back in the room, she spotted Joshua standing with Grace and Paige, who were each holding her nieces in their arms. It seemed as if they were introducing Violet to their girls. Even from this distance, Honor could see it was achingly sweet. She felt a little hitch in her heart. If her own child had lived, he or she might be standing alongside his or her cousins. Her chest tightened as she watched from a distance.

She stood there for a moment, unsure of whether to join the group or walk off to another area. Hazel's

comments were still ringing in her ear. Paige saved her
from having to make that decision for herself.

"Honor! Come see. Isn't this the cutest thing?" Paige
called out, waving her over.

Honor walked over and watched as Emma and Violet gave each other kisses and tightly held hands. They
had made fast friends. It was a bittersweet moment for
Honor. Although it made her feel happy to see Violet
making friends with Emma, thoughts of her own child
raced through her head. She couldn't help but think of
what might have been.

"They're adorable together," Honor said, her eyes
straying toward Joshua. Standing so close to him was
a bit of an assault on her senses. The spicy smell of
his aftershave rose to her nostrils. He was looking at
her with an intensity that made her want to look away
from his gaze. The energy between them was palpable.

"I think it's time we changed some diapers," Grace
said, tugging Paige by the arm and quickly leading
her away. After Grace and Paige made a fast exit, she
and Joshua were standing there together, just the two
of them.

"This is some birthday party," Joshua said, letting
out a low whistle.

Jasper had transformed the eatery into a replica
of a tropical island. There were palm trees, flower
necklaces, grass skirts, tiki torches and pineapple cen-
terpieces. Honor really had the feeling she had been
transported to another world.

"Jasper really outdid himself," Honor said. She was
proud of her grandfather for stepping up to do something spectacular for Hazel. Ever since Honor could
remember, Hazel had been there as a steady, guiding

presence for the Prescott family. She deserved to be the center of attention tonight.

"It's more like a Fourth of July celebration. Someone said there are actually fireworks later on." Joshua's eyes went wide.

Honor giggled. "Hazel is the grand dame of Love. Everything revolves around her," Honor said with a shake of her head. "She deserves it though. I've never met a more gentle, supportive person in my life."

"She's gone out of her way for Theo and me ever since we came back to town. I'm still in awe over the fact that she allowed us to host the reception here. I know she must have called in a lot of favors for that one."

"She always did favor you. It used to drive me crazy in Bible class. She let you get away with everything and anything!" Joshua had been a really cute little kid. He had managed to wrap Hazel completely around his finger.

Joshua threw back his head and laughed. "Spoken by the princess of Love. Everyone in this town always adored you. They all thought butter wouldn't melt in your mouth."

She scoffed at the notion. "There was always too much tomboy in me to be a princess."

"That's what made me fall in love with you," he said in a low voice. "You knew how to ride Lola bareback in the morning and go for a manicure in the afternoon."

Violet reached out and grabbed Honor's necklace. Joshua gently admonished Violet and extricated her chubby little fingers from the gold chain.

"Sorry about that," he apologized. "She loves shiny, sparkly things."

"Joshua. Can I hold her?" she asked, wanting desperately to hold the precious little bundle in her arms.

A huge grin broke out on his face. "Of course you can." He transferred Violet into Honor's arms. "You look like you know what you're doing, that's for sure."

"I have two nieces and a nephew, with another one on the way. I've got skills," she said, gently swaying from side to side. Violet was studying Honor's face, her big blue eyes taking it all in. She raised her hands and place them on either side of Honor's face. She leaned in and placed a kiss on Honor's cheek.

Joshua chuckled. "She really likes you. She's fairly stingy with her kisses."

Honor thought her heart might crack into a million little pieces.

Violet was Joshua's child. In many ways, it was the closest thing to the child she had lost. A baby she had never been able to hold, or rock to sleep, or soothe at bedtime. Tears pricked her eyes. She blinked them away. It was embarrassing for Joshua to witness her being so emotional about his daughter.

"Are you all right?" Joshua asked. His voice sounded tender, which made her want to sob.

"I'm fine," she said, sniffing away tears. There was no way she could tell him the truth about their child. There was too much water under the bridge for her to resurrect it. "I just feel honored to be holding your daughter." Surprise flashed in Joshua's eyes.

All of a sudden a loud clinking noise rang out in the café. Jasper stood up on a bench and looked out over the crowd.

"Attention, everyone. Attention. I have a few words to say about the birthday girl." The guests gathered around Jasper. Hazel made her way through the crowd until she was standing near her husband.

"I want to wish my lovely wife, Hazel, a happy and blessed birthday. Before Hazel came into my life, I was getting by just fine. I was content. But then something wonderful happened. I looked at her one day and realized that she held my heart in the palm of her hand. I wanted to be her guy. Forever. And thankfully, she let me put a ring on her finger."

Everyone began to cheer loudly.

"Wishing you many more birthdays, Hazel," Jasper said, dipping his head down to place a kiss on his wife's lips.

As Hazel and Jasper kissed, the guests thunderously clapped. Honor wiped away a stray tear. This was what she wanted. Real, enduring love. Life wasn't an easy road to navigate. Her grandfather and Hazel were a testament to true, abiding love. They were far from perfect, but they were perfectly made for each other. Their love story was unique.

When Jasper came up for air, he shouted out, "Everyone head outside for the fireworks in celebration of my sweetheart's birthday."

"I love fireworks," Honor gushed.

"I'm not sure Violet will enjoy it," Joshua said. "She doesn't like loud noises. It might startle her."

Honor felt a stab of disappointment. It was nice to spend time with Joshua in a relaxed setting where they weren't fussing about injunctions and the sale of Bud's ranch. She'd forgotten how good it felt just to talk to him. For once her brothers weren't glaring at Joshua and creating an uncomfortable vibe. Something told her she had Paige and Grace to thank for reining her brothers in.

"That's a good point. I always forget how kids and dogs react to fireworks," Honor said, trying to hide her disappointment.

"Go ahead and join the festivities, Honor. Don't worry about us. We'll be fine staying behind," Joshua said.

Grace, who was standing beside them, turned in their direction.

"Joshua. Why don't you let Violet stay with me back here at the café? Eva is way too young for fireworks and I'm watching Emma as well so Paige and Cameron can enjoy the fireworks."

"Are you sure it wouldn't be too much for you?" Joshua asked. "Three little ones can be a handful."

"Of course I'm sure," Grace said with a dismissive wave of her hand. "I've got eyes in the back of my head."

"That's nice of you, Grace," Joshua said, grinning at her. "I'll take you up on the offer."

"Sure thing," Grace said, reaching out for Violet, who easily went into the crook of her arm. With a girl on each hip, Grace said, "Go on and enjoy the fireworks. I'll set the kids up in the back room. Cameron keeps a playpen and toys and blankets in there. It'll be a party for the baby and toddler set."

After grabbing their coats, Joshua and Honor walked outside to Jarvis Street and followed the other guests as they walked over to the town green. Honor and Joshua walked side by side down the street. A few of the towns-folk openly stared at them. Honor was past the point of caring. She wanted to be on civil terms with Joshua. It felt good to know that they'd managed to push past the drama and the conflict, if only for this moment in time.

The sound of fireworks exploding in the sky above them rent the air. Honor let out a gasp as a myriad of colors lit up the onyx sky. Greens and reds. Purples and whites. Threads of silver and gold. She gazed up at the sky, marveling at the fiery beauty of the explosion of colors.

"It's spectacular, isn't it?" Honor asked, turning toward Joshua. He wasn't looking up at the fireworks. He was staring at her, his eyes full of an intensity that made her shiver.

"I can't argue with you on that," he drawled. "You are spectacular, Honor Prescott. You always have been."

Honor let the compliment wash over her. It felt nice to hear it from Joshua's lips. Back in the day he had used his silver tongue to court her, and she'd quickly fallen for his smooth delivery and boyish charm. She felt butterflies tumbling around in her belly. She should be guarding her heart against the threat Joshua represented, but all she wanted to do in this moment was revel in his company and bask in his sweet compliment. No other man had the ability to make her feel the way Joshua did.

As fireworks continued to burst in the sky up above, they stood side by side with their arms touching, watching the brilliant pyrotechnic display. As it died down, folks began to meander away from the town green.

"Let's take the long way back," Joshua suggested. "It'll give me an opportunity to take a walk down memory lane and check out the new additions to this area. I really haven't had an opportunity to explore."

"Okay," Honor agreed, stuffing her mittened hands in her jacket pockets as they headed toward Jarvis Street. The temperature had dipped down, making it much colder than it had been this afternoon. "There are a few changes here in town you might not have seen yet."

"Looking forward to it," Joshua said. "Bud used to talk my ear off about Hazel's boot company and the cannery that never opened. He really loved this town."

"And we loved him back. I used to enjoy it when he would come sit with me for a cup of coffee at the Moose Café. He would just saunter over and sit with me at my table." She let out a ragged sigh. "I miss his sly sense of humor and his knock-knock jokes. They were terrible, but I pretended to love each and every one of them."

"That was awfully sweet of you. Theo and I used to tell him not to give up his day job because he was never going to make it as a comedian."

They both laughed as the memories of Bud Ransom washed over them like a cool spring rain.

"That was a pretty great speech Jasper made about Hazel. I have to admit, I didn't think he had it in him. He always struck me as the curmudgeon type."

Honor smirked. "Jasper is full of surprises. And marriage to Hazel has truly enriched his life. It's really been gratifying to watch their love story unfold."

"It reminds me of my grandparents. Bud lost a huge chunk of himself when my grandmother died. They were soul mates."

"Speaking of marriage, you never wanted to remarry and give Violet a mother?" she asked. She must be a glutton for punishment for even inquiring. It hurt to imagine Joshua with a wife and family.

"Not really. Of course I've thought about it, but I want something that's built to last," he answered with a shrug. "Lauren and I didn't make it very long. Our marriage was a train wreck. I would love for Violet to have a mother, but I certainly don't want a second marriage to fail."

"I'm sorry. It must have been painful to go through that," she said, her mind whirling with questions. Their marriage had been short-lived, yet they had clearly re-united years later and conceived Violet. Although she yearned to ask Joshua that very thing, Honor didn't feel she had the right to probe.

"You're probably wondering about Violet, huh?" he asked.

She let out a sigh of relief. "To be honest, I am. Bud said you got married not that long after you left Love. There are some gaps in the story I can't quite figure out. The timing doesn't add up."

"You're right. I met Lauren in Singapore about four months after I left town. She was over there with her parents who were missionaries. We got married after a whirlwind courtship, then set up house as soon as we landed stateside." He clenched his teeth. "It was fool-ish on both our parts. She was getting over someone who'd been killed in the army." He locked gazes with Honor. "And I was still very much in love with you."

Her stomach tensed. Joshua was basically telling her he had married his ex-wife on the rebound. It made her heart ache to hear it. At the very same time, Honor had been struggling to get over him and mourning the loss of their child.

Her throat felt dry. "Did you ever love her?"

He shook his head. "I cared about Lauren and I thought I was in love with her, but I don't think either of us truly loved each other. Not in the truest sense of the word. If we did, I think we would have fought harder to stay together. It didn't even come close to the way I felt about you."

Something flickered between them. An electric pulse hummed and crackled in the air. Honor could almost feel her heart swelling inside her chest.

Honor frowned. "But clearly you must have reunited with Lauren when Violet was conceived?"

"There's something I didn't tell you about Violet," Joshua said, a hint of strain in his voice. He hesitated for a moment. "It will probably answer all your questions. She's not my biological child."

Honor gasped. He could see the surprise on her lovely face. Her blue-gray eyes widened. Her lips parted. Joshua could see the questions emanating from her eyes.

"Lauren and I stayed in touch after the divorce. Every now and again she would drive from Tacoma to see me and we would go to church together or eat at a nice Italian restaurant. She even introduced me to her boyfriend once. I got the impression she was looking for my approval. I didn't hesitate to give it to her, Honor. He seemed like a good enough guy and I wanted her to be happy. She wanted the same for me.

"About a year ago, I got a call from her begging me to travel to Tacoma to see her. When I got there,

I noticed two things. She was heavily pregnant and she looked really ill. She had dark shadows under her eyes and she was rail-thin despite her pregnancy. It was alarming."

Honor frowned. "What was wrong with her?"

"She had breast cancer. And she suspended all treatment while she was carrying Violet. More than anything in the world, she wanted a healthy baby. The cancer was very aggressive though. Lauren knew she wasn't going to make it. She was just holding on long enough to deliver her baby girl." He swallowed past the huge lump sitting in his throat. "It turns out her boyfriend dumped her and bailed when he found out she was sick. He refused to step up as a father, so I agreed to assume that role. It gave her the peace she needed before she passed. I've never regretted it for a single second."

She raised a hand to her throat. "Oh, Joshua," Honor said, wiping away stray tears. Sniffling noises emanated from her. "Of course you don't regret it. How could you ever?"

"Honor, she's mine in every way that matters. It's thicker than blood. I chose to be her father. I've been on my own with Violet since she was a few weeks old. I had no clue how to care for a baby or even change a diaper. But I knew I was her father. I loved her from the day she came into this world."

Watching Honor's emotional reaction caused a fierce response inside him. It felt as if his heart was being squeezed inside his chest. He hated to see her cry. He reached out and wiped away a tear as it slid past her lower lid.

Her lips trembled. "Joshua. What an unselfish act!

You didn't have any legal ties to Lauren, but you stepped in to raise her child. If you hadn't done so, she might have ended up in foster care. She's one fortunate little girl."

"To be honest, I think I'm the blessed one. Being Violet's father is the most important role I've ever played. It gave me a shot at redemption for all the rotten things I did here in town. It made me a grown-up."

"I get it. God was watching out for Violet. And you as well. He put the two of you together and now you're a family."

Joshua grinned. "Yes, indeed. Now we're a family. She's my entire world."

"I appreciate you sharing all of it with me. I know it's quite personal."

"So, now that I've told you my story, I have a question for you. Why are you still single?"

Honor bit her lip. "Hmm. That's rather tricky to explain. After I refused to be a part of the Operation Love program, I think the local men gave up on me." She twisted her mouth. "A lot of them are afraid of my brothers. Some folks think they're intimidating." She arched an eyebrow in his direction.

"Hey! I wasn't afraid of them!" Joshua protested, holding up his hands.

Honor giggled and shook her head. "Whatever you say."

"Well, maybe I was a little bit afraid of Boone," he conceded. "He was mean. And he walked around with that gold sheriff's badge on his jacket pocket. From the first time he saw me, your brother didn't like me."

"I don't think that's true, Joshua. To be fair, he only started to dislike you when we began dating."

The Prescott brothers had always been protective of their little sister. She had been the jewel in their crown. As the oldest, Boone had taken it upon himself to act as Honor's guardian. It had driven her crazy to be treated like a child, which had led to many fights between Honor and Boone.

Being a father provided Joshua with insight. He knew without a shadow of a doubt he would protect Violet's heart the same way Boone had tried to safeguard Honor. And Lord help the young man if he acted as wild and foolish as he once had.

"I sure gave him plenty of reasons to dislike me," Joshua said, reflecting on his teenage antics. "It must have been hard to see your boyfriend go head-to-head with your brother so often. Sadly, I never really stopped to consider how my actions affected other people. I wonder sometimes how things might have been different if I had acted accordingly."

"It's impossible to go back and change the past." There was tension laced in Honor's voice. He wondered if she was thinking about what might have been if the circumstances had been different.

He reached for her chin and lifted it up so their gazes locked.

"I'm sorry for every ounce of pain I inflicted on you," he said in a tender voice. "And I hate that we're on opposite sides regarding Bud's estate."

Honor shrugged. "It can't be helped, can it? It's just the way it is."

"I suppose not," he said, gently stroking the line of her jaw with his finger. "Honor Prescott, you're still the most beautiful woman I've ever seen. For the record, any man would be fortunate to have you." His own words served as a reminder of how blessed he'd once felt to have been loved by Honor. "And I know it's been a long time since we've done this, but I'd like to kiss you."

Chapter Eleven

I'd like to kiss you.

It had been a long time since Honor had kissed a man. The last time she had kissed Joshua he'd been more boy than man. If she was being honest with herself, this kiss had been in the back of her mind since she'd first seen him at the ranch a few weeks ago. But with so much standing between them, a kiss had seemed impossible.

Her mouth felt dry. All she could do was nod. He dipped his head down and placed his mouth over hers in a tender, romantic meeting of their lips. He tasted sweet like cinnamon. As his lips moved over hers, Honor wished it could go on forever and ever.

Kissing Joshua felt like coming home. It was familiar and achingly gentle. It took her back to a more innocent time when she had believed in fairy-tale endings and enduring love. Her nostrils were filled with the rich, woodsy scent of him. She raised her hands up and trailed her fingers along the nape of his neck. Her fingers brushed against his hair.

When the kiss ended, Joshua swept his lips against

her temple. His touch was feather light. He threaded his hands through her hair and pulled her back toward him for another kiss. When they finally broke apart, Honor felt breathless.

This is what had been missing from her life for all this time. Sparks. Not a single man had ever made her feel the way Joshua did. This feeling of being one with another person. A connection that withstood separation and pain and disappointment.

Joshua ran his palm against the side of her face. "Honor. You're making me feel like I'm sixteen all over again."

She looked up into his eyes. "I haven't felt like this in a long time. Not since we were together," she whispered.

"I feel the same way," he said, letting out a deep breath.

Fear rose up inside her. Joshua felt something, too. It made it all the more real and frightening. She had been down this road before and gotten terribly hurt in the process. It was like playing with fire. This pull she felt toward Joshua could cause her heartbreak down the road. Sharing a kiss didn't change a thing. There were still huge chasms between them.

For so long Honor had stuffed her emotions down, fearful of cracking into little pieces. She had mourned the loss of Joshua so fiercely that her heart hadn't been able to open itself up to anyone else ever since.

Was she just getting carried away by the moment? She was a very sentimental person. Perhaps that's all this was. Nostalgia over the past and her first love. An inability to close the door on something that had ended a long time ago.

"I can tell your brain is racing with a hundred different thoughts." He reached out and smoothed a spot on her forehead with his fingers. "And this little frown needs to go away. Stop worrying so much."

Honor couldn't think of a single thing to say. She had been worried ever since Joshua stepped foot back in town. It always felt as if raging rivers stood between them. On some level they both knew that this brief interlude would quickly fade away in the harsh light of day. When they each woke up tomorrow morning, nothing will have changed. If the injunction held out, there would be resentment simmering between them. And if the sale of the ranch was approved, Joshua would be leaving Love and returning to the life he'd built in Seattle.

It was best to focus on lighter things. If only for tonight. When Joshua had told her about embracing Violet as his own despite the fact that she wasn't his biological child, Honor had felt a strong urge to tell him about the child they'd lost. But what good would it have done? Much like the rest of their relationship, it was water under the bridge.

"You said that you wanted to see any new additions to town. I have something to show you," Honor said, tugging Joshua by the arm and leading him a few feet down the street.

She stopped in her tracks and pointed at the building. "Look! It's the Free Library of Love. Isn't it magnificent?"

"Wow. It's fantastic," Joshua said as he admired the building. "Love is patient. Love is kind. *Corinthians*." He read the words imprinted on the front of the library.

"Love never fails," Honor said, wishing in her heart

it was true. Love had failed both of them in the past. And here she stood with Joshua in the moonlight having just shared a fantastic embrace with him. She must be all kinds of crazy to have ventured down that road with him again.

"A brand-new library is a great addition to Love," Joshua said, admiring the structure. "I'm not sure if I would have spent a lot of time here as a teenager," he said with a chuckle, "but it's great for the town."

"A lot has changed in six years," she noted. The town of Love had gone through a recession, lost beloved members of their town, created a lucrative company, Lovely Boots, and created the innovative program, Operation Love. They had gone through some difficult times, but the town was still standing. The town of Love had endured. Yet, Joshua had missed all of it. The tragedies and the triumphs. The townsfolk coming together to rebound from financial ruin. And he hadn't been aware of Bud's determination to bequeath the Diamond R to his beloved hometown.

Both she and Joshua had changed. They were no longer the high school sweethearts who had been head over heels in love with one another. They were two strong-willed people who might be headed for a legal showdown in court over Bud's property. They didn't believe in the same things. She sighed. No matter how fantastic their kiss had been, it couldn't alter reality.

"It really has," he agreed with a nod. He locked gazes with her, his eyes filled with intensity.

Honor bowed her head. She was beginning to think kissing Joshua hadn't been such a good idea. Looking into Joshua's eyes complicated matters. They were pulling her in. "We should be getting back. Violet will be looking for you," she said in a brisk tone.

He nodded his agreement. They began to walk down Jarvis Street toward the Moose Café. Joshua's mood seemed contemplative. Perhaps he, too, was coming to the realization that the kiss between them had only served to complicate an already messy situation.

Silence reigned as they walked back toward the café. From this point forward, Honor was determined to avoid being alone with Joshua. She didn't need any more trips down memory lane with him or tender kisses in the moonlight. Joshua had the ability to make her forget all of the reasons why they shouldn't be kissing in the first place.

Honor needed to focus instead of getting distracted by Joshua. She wasn't going to allow a tender kiss to deter her from the main objective—preventing the Ransom brothers from selling the Diamond R to the Alloy Corporation. If Joshua Ransom thought he had softened her up tonight with his boyish charms, he had another think coming.

On the ride home to the ranch after Hazel's party, Joshua had plenty of time to reflect on his impulsive decision to kiss Honor. Kissing her had been an act of sheer nerve on his part. And, although it had felt good in the moment, he was having deep regrets. Honor wasn't the type of woman a man should casually kiss. Everything about her screamed home, hearth and forever. But he couldn't give her any of those things. Their one shot at a happy ending had fallen apart six years ago. He clenched his jaw and let out a ragged sigh. It had been foolish to give in to nostalgia. There wasn't a single thing tying them together in the present.

Theo kept giving him curious sideways glances. He knew his brother wanted to ask him about his mood, but so far Theo hadn't peppered him with any questions.

He began tapping his fingers on the steering wheel. Suddenly, he was a bundle of nervous energy. Irritation bubbled up inside him. If he had been alone in the truck, Joshua knew he might roar with frustration. Life wasn't fair.

Theo grumbled. "All right, already. What's up with you tonight?"

Joshua feigned ignorance. He didn't need Theo coming down on him about the foolishness of kissing Honor. His brother had made it clear years ago he didn't care for her. Theo had always believed Honor hadn't loved him as much as he'd loved her. And he had been of the belief that they had been way too young to commit to a future together.

"I'm just tired. It's been a long day."

Theo scoffed. "Gimme a break, Joshua. I've known you all your life. It's not simply fatigue. Fess up."

Joshua sighed. "Honor and I shared a special moment." He was trying to be discreet, while at the same time letting his brother know they'd connected in a meaningful way. Joshua needed someone he could trust to confide in.

"A special moment?" Theo asked. "What does that mean?"

"I kissed her," he blurted out. "And she kissed me back."

Theo began to mutter in an angry tone. "What in

the world did you do that for? Are you a glutton for punishment or what?"

"Whoa! Take it easy. Haven't you ever acted on impulse?"

Theo shook his head and muttered angrily. "Why are you doing this to yourself? She demolished your heart six years ago. What do you think is going to happen this time around? Roses and moonlight?"

Joshua looked away from the road for a quick moment, shooting Theo a deadly glare. "I made a mistake by kissing her. I'm already kicking myself for doing it. If you can't say anything supportive, don't say a word. Okay?"

Silence stretched out between them. The radio was the only sound in the car. Violet was peacefully sleeping in the back seat.

"I'm sorry, Joshua. You know how I am. I shoot from the hip. I'm sorry if it sounded harsh." He quirked his mouth. "I'm only watching out for your best interests. I'm worried about you. And you know I always have your back."

Joshua knew how difficult it was for his brother to apologize. It always had been, ever since they were kids. "It's all right. I know you're trying to protect me, but I've got this under control."

"Do you?" Theo pressed. "Because it seems to me that despite all reason, Honor still has a hold on you. It makes no sense to me! Her main goal is to prevent us from selling the ranch. What happens if the injunction holds and we can't sell the Diamond R?"

Joshua swallowed past the huge lump sitting in his throat. "We'd have to accept it. I would try to see the bigger picture and find meaning in the judge's decision."

"How do you think this town will react if we get the green light to move forward with the sale of the ranch? It won't be pretty."

He felt his jaw tighten. Why was his brother so intent on hammering his point home? It wasn't as if Joshua was dreaming of a happily-ever-after with Honor. Their opposing views on the future of Bud's property represented the huge chasm between them. And he wasn't putting down roots here in Love, no matter what the judge decided.

"They'll rebound from it," he said, answering Theo's question. "This is a town with a lot of faith and fortitude. Love has endured much worse than this. I'm guessing it might not be an ideal outcome, but everyone would learn to live with it, including Honor."

The thought of it caused a tightening sensation to spread across his chest. Honor's face flashed before his eyes and he pushed the thought of her away. He didn't want to think about her being hurt or disappointed. Joshua needed to focus on his own wants and Violet's needs.

"Honestly, we probably won't even have to deal with the fallout. We're not sticking around Love any longer than necessary," Theo said. "If I were you, I would avoid any more tender moments with Honor. It only serves to muddy the waters."

"You're right," he said with a nod. "Things don't need to get any more complicated than they already are."

Try as he might, Joshua couldn't completely snuff out the memory of the kiss he'd shared with Honor.

It was probably the last one he would ever share with his ex-fiancée. Soon enough he and Violet would be back in Seattle, settled into their normal routine. Honor would be nothing more than a bittersweet memory from his past.

As they approached the gates to the Diamond R Ranch, Joshua cast his gaze across the property. Illuminated by the moonlight, it was the most stunning vista he had ever laid his eyes upon. It would always be near and dear to his heart. The memories would have to be enough to sustain him.

Joshua had come back to Love, Alaska, for the sole purpose of tying up his grandfather's estate. Honor Prescott wasn't part of his future. He needed to work harder to put her firmly in the past.

After the guests from Hazel's party dispersed from the Moose Café, Honor stuck around to help with the cleanup. Her staying to pick up the mess allowed Hazel and Jasper to head home without having to worry about the nitty-gritty details. Boone decided to send Grace home with baby Eva so he could stay and help Honor tidy up the place. The Moose Café would be open for breakfast first thing tomorrow morning and they wanted to make sure everything was in pristine condition.

After forty-five minutes or so, they were done. Boone grabbed two sodas from the fridge and sank down onto a seat at one of the tables.

He patted the chair beside him. "Come sit with me. I need to talk to you."

A feeling of panic immediately seized her by the throat. Having a talk with her older brother rarely boded well. More times than not, Boone subjected her to a lecture of epic proportions. She wasn't in the mood tonight.

Boone began to chuckle. "You look like a deer caught in the headlights. I want to talk, not torture you. Have a little faith, sis."

Honor moved toward the table hesitantly. Boone stood up and pulled a chair out for her. She sat down and folded her hands in front of her on the table.

"You look like a little kid sitting like that."

She squirmed in her seat. "I feel like one. I have an idea what this is about."

Boone arched an eyebrow. He sat back in his chair, arms folded across his chest. "Really?"

"It's about Joshua. Am I right?"

"Yes. You are." He stroked his jaw. "There are a few things I'd like to say about you and Joshua."

She slammed her hands down on the table. "Boone, there really isn't anything between Joshua and me other than an uneasy truce. So you can save your speech. I really don't want to hear a lecture from you about how unsuitable we are for each other and how rotten Joshua is. I know you think he's a terrible, irresponsible person. You thought our engagement was the worst thing possible. And I know you must think I'm the biggest fool in the world for ever falling for him all those years ago."

Boone's jaw dropped. "Is that really how I sound?"

"Honestly, yes," Honor admitted in a soft voice.

He reached out and took her hands in his. "I'm so sorry, Honor. It seems I've overplayed my position as eldest brother of the Prescott clan. I only ever wanted to protect my baby sister. I never for a single second ever wanted to clip your wings or make you feel less than for your choices.

"When I met Gracie we were opposites in many ways. Despite everything we fell for each other. Things fell apart when I found out she was lying to me and this town. In the end, I realized that Gracie made a mistake. I forgave her." Boone looked down for a moment. His expression was full of emotion. "We've had it a bit rough, haven't we? Two parents who bailed on us. We've all had to raise each other and rely on ourselves, haven't we?"

The look of pain on her brother's face was enough to bring her to her knees. Boone was a tough guy, one who had never shown a whole lot of emotion, especially about their upbringing. "We did," she said through a haze of tears. "We got through it though. Prescotts are made of strong stuff." She wiped tears away with the back of her hand.

"Here's the thing. Loving Gracie taught me something important. You can't help who you fall in love with. You just can't. When you and Joshua fell in love as teenagers, all I could see was the negative. I was so scared for my little sister I never stopped to appreciate your love story. And when the church burned down, it gave me a legitimate reason to hate him."

Honor's eyes widened. "That's all in the past, Boone."

Boone sighed. "Not really. It's crept into the present. I don't like harboring negative feelings toward people. As a man of faith, it's been a failing of mine. So I decided that I can't do that anymore. I can't hate Joshua for a mistake he made when he was barely of age. I don't want to carry that burden around anymore. It's too heavy."

"Oh, Boone. That's wonderful. Forgiveness is such a powerful gift. Not only for Joshua, but for yourself as well." She reached out and squeezed his hand.

"I was watching you tonight with Joshua while the fireworks were going off. It made me wonder if you still had feelings for him."

Honor bowed her head. "I'll always have the memories of what we shared, but that's all in the past. As it stands now, we're on opposite sides of this issue regarding the Diamond R. Joshua can't wait to head back to Seattle and put this town in his rearview mirror. There's no way things could ever work out between us. Even if the injunction holds, it's still a messy situation."

"I just wanted to let you know that I'll support you, no matter what. I didn't have your back six years ago, and I know it caused you a lot of pain."

"That means a lot to me," she said, fighting back tears.

"Now, if he decides not to sell the ranch to the Alloy Corporation, that might change things between you. Am I right?"

Honor frowned. "I don't think he will, Boone. He's made no secret of his plans."

"I'm really sorry to hear that. It would be a blessing if he changed his mind," Boone said. "For all our sakes."

She jutted her chin up. "It would be wonderful, but I learned a long time ago not to hope for the impossible." She felt exhaustion sweep through her. The entire situation was taking a heavy toll on her.

"Oh, Honor," Boone said in a voice clogged with emotion. "I'm so sorry."

Something about Boone's tone caused her to crack

wide open. Honor got up from her seat and threw herself against Boone's chest. She began to cry—tears of frustration and loss. She had no idea what might happen to the Diamond R, but Honor knew that she and Joshua were hopelessly at odds over it. Filing the injunction had been a long shot, and even though no decision had yet been made, she could almost sense that it wouldn't hold up.

Joshua and Theo would sell Bud's beloved ranch to developers. The Diamond R would cease to exist as they had always known it. And Joshua and Violet would head back to their lives in Seattle. The very thought of it made her heart ache way more than she wanted to acknowledge.

Chapter Twelve

Joshua gazed out the window of Bud's study. The ranch was blanketed in white, with a recent snowfall leaving the ground packed with snow. Everything was white, for as far as the eye could see. A few of the ranch hands were leading horses into the paddock. Maybe he would bring Violet outside later on to play in the snow. He was in an antsy mood. Last night he had tossed and turned for hours, torn apart by the moral dilemma over the Diamond R. Selling the ranch and returning to Seattle was the only thing that made sense. But every time he thought about going through with the sale he felt sick to his stomach.

Theo walked into the study, his face lit up with a huge grin. "I just got the call. The judge has lifted the injunction," he announced in a voice full of triumph. He raised his fist in the air and shook it.

Joshua knew he should be feeling on top of the world at the moment. Hadn't this been what he'd been waiting to hear? Why wasn't he rejoicing? All he felt was emptiness.

"Did you hear me? It's over. We can sell Bud's property to whomever we choose." Theo was practically jumping up and down with joy at the news.

"I heard you," he said. "It's a lot to take in."

Theo narrowed his gaze as he looked at him. "It's a victory, Joshua. We're one step closer to leaving this town behind us." Theo shook his head at Joshua. "I'm beginning to think you were hoping we would lose." Theo glared at him, then stormed out of the room.

Joshua sighed raggedly. The legal victory had hit him like a ton of bricks. He hadn't been expecting to hear anything definitive today. Instead of rejoicing, his head was filled with Honor. He had no idea whether or not she'd received word about the injunction. The news couldn't have come at a worse time. She was scheduled to come to the ranch this morning to check up on the calves, as well as some other livestock. One of the calves seemed to have taken a turn for the worse. Joshua had called Honor to let her know about the situation.

He had no intention of telling her about the injunction being lifted. It would only cause more strain between them.

While Winnie tended to Violet, Joshua found himself listening for any signs of Honor's arrival at the ranch. He was pacing back and forth in the den when he heard the crunch of tires from outside. One glance out of the window confirmed Honor's arrival. He quickly put on his parka and headed outside to greet her.

She was just getting out of her car when he reached her side. Dressed in a pair of nice-fitting jeans and a snug winter parka, Honor looked casual yet lovely. The gray knit hat perched on her head gave her a wholesome look. Joshua stuffed down a wild impulse to kiss her. But he knew it wasn't his place to do so. It would only serve to make things messier than they already were, he reckoned.

"Honor. Thanks for coming over."

"Of course. I came as soon as I could. What's going on with the calf?"

"It hasn't been eating or moving all that much. It doesn't seem to be thriving."

Honor nodded. There were crease lines around her mouth and eyes. He knew she took her job seriously. The welfare of animals was of the utmost importance to her. Part of her profession involved wildlife rehabilitation.

They took off toward the barn with Honor leading the way. She made a quick beeline to the area where the calves were situated. He didn't need to tell Honor which calf was doing poorly. It was evident by the way she sat off to the side, not interacting with the other calves.

Joshua stood and watched as Honor gently examined the calf. After a few minutes, her shoulders slumped. She turned toward him. "You were right. She's not doing well. It could be dehydration or a virus, although I would think if it was viral the others would be doing poorly as well. I'm not a vet, so you might want another opinion, but it's not looking good." She shrugged. "She needs special care. There's not a whole lot we can do if she continues to struggle." She bowed her head.

"Honor. Don't feel bad. Sometimes it's just nature's way. You've been incredible. You've got such a nurturing instinct with animals and with people. You'll make a great mother one day."

Honor looked up at him with tears swimming in her eyes. She held up her hand. "Please don't say that," she said, her voice quivering.

Goose bumps raised up on the back of his neck. There was something going on with Honor that surpassed her worry about the calf. Clearly, his comment about motherhood had struck a nerve. He needed to know what was going on with her. Had he done something?

"What is it?" he asked. "What did I say to upset you like this?" A sudden tension hummed and pulsed in the air between them.

"I was a mother, Joshua," she said, swiping away tears with her fingers. "For a brief moment in time I was pregnant with a child. Our child!"

"I suffered a miscarriage." Finally, after all these years it felt good to say the words out loud. She had been carrying this secret for such a long time.

Joshua's jaw went slack. He let out an agonized sound. "Honor. When did it happen? You never said a word."

"It was shortly after I arrived at college. I was under a lot of stress and I hadn't told anyone about the pregnancy. By that time, I had no idea where you were or what you were doing. When I lost the baby, I figured it no longer mattered."

Tears pooled in his eyes. "I'm so sorry. I wish I'd known. I'm so sorry you had to go through that type of pain. It guts me to know you had to go through all of it alone."

She winced as painful memories swept over her. Honor hadn't told a single person about the pregnancy or subsequent miscarriage. "And I was all alone to deal with it. I didn't have a single person to confide in or to cry on their shoulder."

"I wish I could've helped you through it," Joshua said. She could hear the agony laced in his voice. "We could have mourned the loss together."

Why hadn't she confided in Paige or Ruby or Hazel about her pregnancy? She had felt such shame. As an unmarried woman, Honor had felt ashamed about conceiving a child. She and Joshua had both been struggling a bit with their faith at the time of conception. Neither had lived up to the values of their faith by having sex without the benefit of marriage. Although it had been a mistake to do so, Honor had dearly loved her baby. She had been committed to raising the child with love and faith. It had all been ripped away from her in the most devastating way.

"Honor, please. Let me hold you," Joshua begged. "I don't want you to carry the weight of this on your shoulders. I can carry the burden from now on." Tears were streaming down his face. She could see how much pain he was in. It mirrored her own emotions.

Joshua reached for her and pulled her into his arms. She felt almost weightless. For so long she had been holding this secret close to the vest. Finally, she was able to share it with the person who should have known from the beginning. Her baby's father. Joshua's strong arms held her tightly. She relaxed against him, giving in to the need to be comforted.

All of a sudden, Theo was standing at the stall entrance, his expression somber as he looked back and forth between them. She pulled away from Joshua.

"Oh, I'm sorry. I didn't know you were here, Honor," Theo said, his eyes widening as he looked back and forth between them. With her tearstained face, Honor knew she must look like a mess.

She ducked her head down, feeling embarrassed that Theo had seen her in such an emotional state.

"I'm sorry you're upset, Honor. I guess you heard the news?" Theo asked, looking at Honor with sympathy radiating from his eyes.

"Theo!" Joshua said in a sharp voice. "It's really not a good time."

"What news?" Honor swung her gaze back and forth between the brothers.

Theo's eyes widened. "She doesn't know?"

"I'll tell her in my own time!" Joshua said, furious that Theo had barged in and practically blurted out the information about the injunction.

"I'm sorry. I never meant to butt in," Theo said, quickly retreating and leaving the room.

As soon as he left the room, Honor took a step away from Joshua. She looked at him with suspicion radiating from the depths of her eyes. "What's going on? Theo isn't very subtle. What was he getting at?"

There was no point in hiding it any longer. Honor would find out before the day was done. "The judge rescinded the injunction. As of this afternoon, we're free to sell the Diamond R to whomever we choose."

A shell-shocked expression crept over her face. "I—I can't believe it," she said, stammering. "I was so sure we were on the right side of things."

"I'm sorry," Joshua said. "I know how disappointed you must be."

Her expression was one of utter disbelief. Joshua felt a pang in his heart. She was clearly crushed. It killed him to see her like this. This felt like anything but a victory.

Dear Lord. Please help me find the right words to buoy her spirits. I never wanted her to feel deflated or to feel defeated. It hurts to see her so incredibly wounded. Honor is tough, but at this moment she looks as if she's ready to shatter. Please let me be the one to help her pick up the pieces.

She bowed her head and didn't meet his gaze. Honor raised her hand to her temple. "I really need to go home. I'll write up some instructions for the calf and send them over. I'm not feeling so great." She turned away from him and reached for her bag.

"Honor, please don't leave. Let's talk this out."

Honor turned and faced him. Her cheeks were red and her eyes were rimmed with moisture. She looked away from him.

"Let's face it. There's nothing really to discuss. You won. You can now sell Bud's ranch and head back to Seattle with the proceeds. You should be rejoicing. Isn't this what you wanted?"

His mouth felt dry. The truth was he had wanted the injunction to be lifted, but not at the expense of Honor. Not if it meant he would be moving back to Seattle, never to lay eyes on Honor again. Not if it signified the end of them. At the moment, he wasn't certain what he wanted.

"I never wanted us to be at odds with each other. Surely you know that."

She shook her head. "I don't know anything anymore. Everything has turned upside down. I really don't believe this is what your grandfather wanted. And that breaks my heart."

"This is a terrible situation. It doesn't feel right to be on opposing sides."

She frowned. "What does it matter? You're going to leave, aren't you? Please don't think I'm foolish enough to think you're going to stick around Love, especially since you have a buyer lined up to purchase the property." Her voice had now gone up a few pitches. She clenched her jaw. Storm clouds were brewing in her eyes.

"Honor, my life is in Seattle. It's the only home Violet has ever known. I don't have much of a choice."

She bit her lip. "I understand. But, considering everything, I think it's best you find someone else to check up on the animals from now on. I can't bear to come back here knowing what's going to happen to the Diamond R."

"Please don't say that." It felt like Honor was slipping out his life yet again. He couldn't explain why, but it left him feeling completely bereft.

"Why not? It's the truth!" she snapped.

She zipped up her coat, then jammed her hat back on her head.

Joshua reached out and gently grasped her by the arm. She shook him off and backed away from him.

Her mouth was a hard, thin line. "I'm sorry, Joshua. There's really nothing left to be said."

Joshua felt numb as he watched Honor run toward her car as if her feet were on fire. She couldn't get away from him fast enough. And given what she had just found out about the injunction being lifted, he couldn't say he blamed her.

He was still reeling about Honor's miscarriage. She had been forced to deal with the pregnancy and the monumental loss of their child all by herself. So many things were weighing heavily on him at the moment. Anger and frustration rose up inside him.

He stormed into the house, eager to confront his brother. Theo had somehow managed to make a bad situation worse. And he couldn't help but wonder if his brother had done it on purpose to put an even deeper wedge between him and Honor. Theo was sitting in the study at Bud's desk, riffling through a stack of papers.

"Thanks for making a mess of things," Joshua said in a raised voice.

Theo twisted his mouth. "It wasn't on purpose, Joshua. Take it easy. She was going to find out sooner or later."

"Why did you come barging in like that?" Joshua asked. "Did you honestly not know she was here? Her car was parked right outside the house. Surely you saw it."

"I can't believe you're angry at me. We should be celebrating our legal victory and all you can think of is the precious Prescott princess."

Joshua stepped toward his brother. They were standing eye to eye. He was bristling with rage. "Watch yourself, Theo. Don't say a word against Honor. She's innocent in all of this."

Theo sneered. "Are you kidding me? Honor set this whole thing in motion by filing that injunction." He let out a harsh sounding laugh. "What makes you think she's the victim?"

"She didn't do it to be malicious. Honor has principles she lives by, Theo. Her whole professional life revolves around wildlife and land preservation. It actually tears her apart to think about the desecration of Bud's property. Is that something you've even thought about once?"

Theo wrinkled his nose. "What's wrong with you? Are you changing your mind about selling the ranch?" he asked.

Joshua knit his brows together. "No. Yes. I don't know," he moaned. "Ever since we came back here, my head has been spinning. Half the time I don't know if I'm coming or going."

Theo's expression softened. "Is this about Honor? Why is it that all roads lead back to her? You were kids when you got engaged. It was a lifetime ago. You need to let go of it already. Put it in your rearview mirror."

"Don't you think I've tried? I've spent six years trying to move past all the painful things that happened in this town. It wasn't easy rebuilding my life, but I did it. For some reason, I still can't move past Honor. And I know it's crazy and pointless, because she can't deal with the fact that we're selling the ranch. She'll hate me for it." He bowed his head down. "I wish I'd come clean with her all those years ago about the fire. Things might be very different today if I had."

Theo gazed at him with sad eyes. "I'm so sorry you're in pain, Joshua. You deserve happiness more than anyone I've ever known."

Joshua shrugged. Hadn't he been a happy man before his return to Love? Maybe he should have just stayed put in Seattle and skipped all of the drama.

All of a sudden he felt defeated. Crushed. His conscience was eating at him. Honor's words kept replaying in his mind, over and over again. They nagged at him relentlessly.

For what shall it profit a man if he shall gain the whole world and lose his own soul? If he moved forward and sold the Diamond R Ranch, Joshua feared he would regret it for the rest of his life.

Chapter Thirteen

Honor wasn't sure how she made it back to the wildlife center in one piece. She had sobbed the entire drive from the Diamond R Ranch. It broke her heart to know that the Diamond R was going to be desecrated. The more she cried, the more she realized that she wasn't simply upset over the injunction being lifted. Joshua was leaving Love. In all likelihood, she would never see him again. The sale of the Diamond R would permanently sever all of his ties to Love. And, by extension, to her.

It was now hitting her all at once. She hadn't just been fighting the sale of the Diamond R. Honor had been unwilling to let go of Joshua. She had been fighting it tooth and nail.

What a fool she'd been to actually believe he might change his mind about the Diamond R. Her feelings for him had made an idiot of her once again. Joshua was going to sell the ranch for a large sum, then leave town so he could continue his life in Seattle. Just like the last time, Honor would be left behind to lick her wounds.

She shook her head, trying to make sense of the

events of the past few weeks. Her prayers regarding the Diamond R Ranch had been all for naught. Everything was slipping through her fingers. She had failed Bud. Joshua would be leaving town again. And it hurt even more than the first time.

Lord, please help me. Give me the strength to deal with the pain of losing Joshua all over again. Grant me the grace to let go of him, once and for all.

The sound of someone knocking heavily on her door brought her out of her thoughts. She hoped Joshua hadn't followed her back to the wildlife center. There really wasn't anything else left to say. Everything was pretty cut-and-dried. As a result, she felt incredibly empty.

Honor moved toward her front door and wrenched it open. For a moment she thought it was Joshua standing at her doorstep. She quickly realized it was Theo. Although the resemblance between the brothers was startling, Honor had always seen a lot more kindness on Joshua's face.

Seeing Theo standing on her doorstep was surprising. He had never been a member of the Honor Prescott fan club. Most of the time he'd looked straight through her like glass.

"I just need a few minutes if you can spare it," Theo said, his expression intense.

"This isn't a good time," she told him.

What could Theo possibly have to say to her? Hadn't he already crowed about the injunction being lifted? Had he come over to rub her nose in it?

"I really need to speak to you, Honor. This is very important."

Honor sighed, exasperated. "All right, Theo, but

please make it quick." She ushered him inside toward the living room.

"Take a seat," she said, waving him toward the sofa.

"I'd rather stand if it's all right with you. I won't be staying long," Theo said. He took a deep breath. "My brother is a good man. One of his best qualities is his loyalty. If he makes a vow to do something he'll uphold it, even when doing so causes him to lose everything."

She shrugged. "Why are you telling me this?"

He clenched his jaw. "It was all my fault."

Honor frowned. "What are you talking about?"

"The church fire. I started it by playing around with a lighter and a hymnal. I was young and selfish. I was heading back to the army and I knew my service would be negatively impacted if word got out that I started a fire that demolished a church."

She let out a strangled sound. "So Joshua was innocent?"

Theo nodded. His expression was somber. "Joshua was with me, but he had nothing to do with the blaze that burned out of control. It all happened so quickly I was powerless to stop it. I was immature and reckless. Joshua stepped up and volunteered to take the blame once he was identified as the culprit. He could have pointed the finger at me, but he claimed responsibility for the fire. I know it sounds crazy, but he came up with the idea on his own." Theo ran a hand over his face. "As the older brother I should have protected him by telling him it was out of the question. It was my job to watch out for him. But I felt desperate."

"So you let him take the blame?" Honor asked. Although she still felt a little bit dazed by the news, it was slowly starting to sink in. Joshua had been innocent of the charges! And Theo had benefited immensely from Joshua's sacrifice.

Theo bowed his head. "I did. Because of the close resemblance between us, Zachariah Cummings mistook me for Joshua. It wasn't unusual for people to get us confused. So when Zachariah initially reported it to law enforcement, it was Joshua's name he put out there. Everything just spiraled out of control after that. Even though I wanted to take responsibility…I didn't. I left town to return to the army." Theo winced. "Joshua was left holding the bag."

She felt an all-encompassing rage take hold of her. "How could you? You were the older brother. You should have protected him."

"I know, Honor. And even though it's six years too late, that's why I'm here. It's what I'm trying to do now. I reckon your future with Joshua was a casualty of that lie. Joshua would never rat me out by telling you what really happened, but I needed to right that wrong."

"I respect your telling me the truth, but the past is behind us. I'm through with allowing it to have such a strong hold over me. What we had was a youthful romance."

"Are you saying you don't have any feelings for Joshua?" Theo pressed.

Honor raised a hand to massage her forehead. She had a raging headache. Everything was weighing heavily on her. "Does it matter? Too many things are standing between us. Not just the past, but the present as well."

Theo rocked back on his booted feet. "But don't you see, Honor? If he hadn't taken the blame for my actions, the two of you might still be together."

Honor could hear the agony in Theo's voice. He

must have been carrying this guilt around with him for years. Although she and Theo had never been on the same page about anything, Honor's heart went out to him. It was impossible for Theo to go back in time and change the decisions he'd made in the past. Now he just had to find a way to live with it.

"I appreciate your coming here, Theo, but it doesn't change anything. You're still selling the ranch. Joshua still plans to head back to Seattle with Violet. There's nothing I can do to change those things." She wouldn't even know how to go about doing so.

Theo threw his hands up in the air. "Joshua is a great man and an even better brother. He stepped up and claimed Violet as his daughter even though they don't share a single strand of DNA. He's grown into the type of man people look up to and admire. You fought us over the future of the Diamond R. Why are you so willing to roll over and play dead when it comes to fighting for my brother?"

Honor's jaw dropped. Theo was being mighty presumptuous to assume she held romantic feelings for Joshua. Her heart was beating fast. Her palms were sweaty.

She yearned to give him a piece of her mind, but she was done fighting. Honor was all worn-out. At this point in her life she wanted to move forward. She wanted tranquility. Being with Joshua wouldn't give her that. They would always be fighting over Bud's property or the actions of the developers. She would always wonder about the child they'd lost. Some wounds couldn't heal. It was too messy.

"I think it's time I left," Theo said. "Just some food for thought."

Theo nodded at her and strode toward the door. He hesitated a moment at the threshold, then turned to face her. "Pride is a powerful thing, but so is love."

Before she knew it, Theo had made his way toward his vehicle. She sucked in a deep breath. His parting words left her reeling. Was she being prideful? In her opinion it was a matter of being realistic. A person could only surmount so many obstacles. She could only withstand so much pain.

Honor now knew without a shadow of a doubt that she was in love with Joshua. Always had been. Always would be. Finding out the truth about the fire had driven home the point she had always known. Joshua was a good man.

Despite the way he had always been regarded here in town, Joshua had evolved into a wonderful man. He had raised Violet as his own and protected Theo by taking responsibility for the terrible mistake his brother had made. And she would have to love him from a distance, because Joshua would soon be nothing more than a memory.

All she knew at this moment was the ache of her heart shattering into tiny little pieces.

Joshua's thoughts were full of Honor. Every time he'd looked at Violet this afternoon he couldn't help but think of the child Honor had lost. Their child. She had been forced to deal with the heartbreaking situation on her own, with no one to turn to for comfort. The very thought of it made him sick to his stomach. He should have been there to help the woman he loved through the loss of their baby. His mind kept whirling with thoughts of what might have been. What if he hadn't taken the fall for Theo? Would they have stayed together? Or would it all have fallen apart anyway?

It was all so crushing. He should have been there to help Honor shoulder her grief. Joshua should have held her in his arms and mourned alongside her. His faith told him God was in control, but for some reason, that knowledge didn't soothe him. It didn't make it any less agonizing.

He had come out to the stables to spend some time with the horses and to clear his head. He'd almost considered riding Blaze, but his heart wasn't in it at the moment. As he stood in Blaze's stall brushing her coat, Joshua prayed for closure. How could he go back to his life in Seattle with so many issues pressing on his heart?

Lord, I'm really hurting right now. And so is Honor. I never imagined coming back to Love would be such an emotional experience. I thought I could come back to Love, handle my grandfather's affairs and go back to Seattle without skipping a beat. But there are so many things weighing on me right now. If I'm doing the right thing by selling the Diamond R, why do I feel so bad about it?

"I've been looking for you everywhere." He hadn't even heard Theo's footsteps, but here his brother stood a few feet away from him. Theo's brow was furrowed with concern as he gazed at Joshua. "You look like you're in agony."

Joshua looked at Theo through a haze of pain. He didn't even bother to deny it. "That's a good word for it." He let out a tremendous shudder. His shoulders heaved with the effort. "When we arrived here in town everything seemed so crystal clear. But, in a matter of weeks, it's clouded over. I don't know what's right anymore. And I'm afraid if we sell the Diamond R, I won't know who I am any longer."

"You don't want to sell the ranch, do you?" Theo asked. "You didn't give me a straight answer earlier."

Joshua had spent a lifetime trying not to disappoint his older brother. He had always been the classic younger brother looking for Theo's approval. After all these years, he was still yearning for it. He bowed his head. "I don't, Theo. Honestly, I've struggled with the notion ever since the offer was made to us. I can honestly say I don't think it's the right thing to do. It's not in keeping with our grandfather's ideals."

Theo didn't say anything for a few moments. Joshua looked up and met his brother's gaze. As usual, they could easily communicate without a word being spoken. Theo let out a sigh. "All right then, we won't sell. I can't see myself living back here in Love and running the ranch, but from the looks of it, this lifestyle fits you like a glove."

Joshua couldn't believe his ears. "Theo! Are you serious? You were so determined to sell the ranch. What's changed?"

"Seeing you so torn up about everything has forced me to take a good look at myself. The Diamond R is Bud's legacy. It wouldn't work for me to stay here and run it, but I could easily picture you doing it. After all the sacrifices you've made for me, Joshua, it's the least I could do for you and Violet. Money isn't everything."

Joshua ran a shaky hand across his face. Never in a million years would he have imagined things turning on a dime like this. All he could think about was Honor. How would she react to the news? Joshua leaned in and placed his arms around his brother in a warm hug. His gratitude was overflowing.

"What about you and Honor?" Theo asked. "Will this change things?"

Joshua shrugged. "It doesn't change anything. We've never really managed to bridge the gap between us."

Theo reached out and forcibly shook his shoulders. "Joshua! Wake up. You're in love with her. Are you really going to let this opportunity to make things right between the two of you slip through your fingers? Tomorrow isn't promised. We've got to make the most of today. Isn't that what Bud always told us?"

Bud's image flashed before his eyes. Their grandfather had done so much for both of them throughout their lives. He knew without a doubt Bud would want him to fight for his happiness.

"You're right, Theo. I love Honor. I always have. There's nothing I'd like more than to go to her and tell her how I feel, but I have no idea if she feels the same way."

"Really? Because I can see it whenever the two of you are within a ten-mile radius. You love each other."

Joshua felt buoyed up by Theo's words. He was openly saying what Joshua felt in his own heart. It's what he had always known deep down. The love between him and Honor had never been extinguished. Joshua did love her, with every fiber of his being. He had adored her for as long as he could remember. And he knew now he always would.

He smiled at his brother. For the first time in a long time he had reason to hope. "There's love there. I felt it, but I pushed it down because of everything that happened between us in the past. I didn't put my feelings out there due to false pride or fear of getting hurt again. I can't let it go unspoken, especially now that we're keeping the ranch. There's not a single reason we can't be together."

Theo flashed him a grin. "Sounds like you're going to get that happy ending after all." He slapped Joshua on the back.

"I need to go to her, Theo. I haven't told her how I feel. She doesn't know that I'm still in love with her."

"I heard that the town council is holding a meeting. I can't imagine she would miss it." He glanced at his watch. "It starts in about fifteen minutes."

Joshua reached for Blaze's saddle and placed it on his back. He picked up the reins and busied himself placing the bit in the horse's mouth. Then, with one fluid motion, he mounted Blaze.

"Joshua! You're not riding all the way into town on Blaze are you?" Theo asked. "Bud's truck would be a lot faster."

Joshua grinned at him. "Honor fell in love with an Alaskan cowboy. I want to remind her of the fact that I'm still that hometown boy. I've changed in many ways, but I'm still a cowboy, born and bred."

Theo threw back his head and chuckled. "Go get the woman of your dreams, Joshua. Don't worry about Violet. Between me and Winnie, she's in good hands."

Joshua tipped his cowboy hat at his brother and prodded Blaze to get moving. As he galloped across the property and away from the Diamond R Ranch, Joshua felt as if he was soaring. For so long he had told himself he wasn't worthy of a happily-ever-after with Honor. Now he was riding toward a dream he hoped and prayed would come true.

* * *

It hadn't taken long for word to spread around Love about the Ransom brothers' legal victory. The residents were very upset at Bud and his grandsons. Jasper practically had a conniption fit. Honor was grateful for Hazel, who'd managed to calm him down and remind him of his responsibility as town mayor.

"You've got to be calm, cool and collected in the face of adversity," Hazel had reminded him.

"Who says I'm not?" Jasper had roared.

"Experience," Hazel had muttered.

Jasper had decided to call a meeting of the town council in order to address the controversial issue with the entire town. Her brother Boone, as well as Hazel, Paige and Jasper, were members of the town council. Honor knew the event would be heavily attended by the townsfolk. Everyone seemed to have an opinion about the possibility of a dude ranch replacing the Diamond R Ranch. Most were vehemently opposed to it, while a few said it might be good for the town.

Honor arrived early for the town council meeting. She was hoping to meet with Jasper beforehand so she could implore him not to rile up the townsfolk. Bad things happened when people became agitated over things they couldn't control. Honor didn't want Joshua or Theo to be a target of any negativity. She made her way through the throng of people gathered at the town hall. It was standing room only from the looks of it. Thankfully she had asked Ruby to hold a seat for her. She was blessed to have three sisters-in-law who had her back at all times.

When she entered the meeting room, Ruby was standing up toward the front of the room, wildly waving in her direction. Honor rushed toward her so they could sit together.

"This room is really packed," Honor said as she and Ruby hugged by way of greeting each other.

Ruby made a face. "It's insane. Liam stayed home with Aidan tonight. He would hate this crush of people."

"Thanks for saving me a seat, Ruby," Honor said, craning her neck to get a glimpse of the crowd in the back of the room. "I'm fortunate to have even made it inside the room."

"You're welcome," Ruby said. "I'm anxious to hear what everyone has to say."

"Me too," Honor murmured, placing her hand over her belly in order to quiet down the nervous rumbles.

At 5:30 p.m. sharp, Jasper pounded a gavel and called the meeting to order.

"Good evening, friends. We're here tonight to discuss the legal decision rendered regarding the Diamond R Ranch. I'm sure by now you've all heard the news. But for those of you who've been living under a rock, a so-called judge decided that Bud's kin can do what they like with his beloved ranch." Jasper ran a hand over his face. Honor couldn't help but think he looked extremely weary. This issue had taken a toll on him, which was alarming.

"It's an outrage as far as I'm concerned. Poor Bud is probably rolling around in his grave at this development. That man loved this town and he adored his ranch. It meant the world to him. Rumor has it that the ranch will be sold to an outfit of vipers who want to suck the life out of this town." He let out a ragged breath. "All I know is that I've been in constant prayer about it. And I'm not done praying yet. Maybe Theo and Joshua will have a change of heart. I pray they do."

As Jasper sat down, Boone leaned toward him and clapped him on the back. Honor watched as her brother whispered something in her grandfather's ear that made him grin. It lightened Honor's mood to see it. Jasper wasn't as tough as he seemed to be from the outside looking in. He'd been through a lot in his life.

Pastor Jack stepped up to the microphone. "Jasper asked me to be here tonight so I could share some thoughts with you. Bud—bless his heart—didn't leave the town his property. Perhaps there's some meaning there," Pastor Jack said.

"What kind of meaning could there be?" Jasper asked in a raised voice. "The last thing this town needs is a stinkin' dude ranch."

Pastor Jack smiled serenely. "Grace can be found in all types of situations, Jasper. We, as a town, just need to tap into it. This town has been through the best of times and the worst of times. Some of our ancestors searched for gold in the Yukon in the hopes of making it rich and providing for their families. Instead of finding riches, they met with tragedy. Somehow, their families endured. Not too long ago this town was rocked by a financial downturn. Friends became enemies, lovers became estranged. At our worst moment, this town banded together to save ourselves. We endured."

The crowd began to clap thunderously.

Pastor Jack grinned. "If the worst happens and Bud's ranch is transformed into the worst dude ranch in creation, this town won't crumble. We'll endure. As we've always done."

Pastor Jack was right, Honor realized. It wasn't the

end of the world. Dealing with this situation with grace and conviction would go a long way in healing the wounds. She needed to play a role in soothing ruffled feathers rather than riling them up against the legal decision. Love had always endured. It would continue to do so. After all, a town was the sum total of its residents. And the townsfolk here in Love were the best people she had ever known.

As the meeting came to a close and everyone filed outside, Honor felt a feeling of calm wash over her. Snow was gently falling all around them. The air was crisp and biting. The wind was whipping her hair all about her face.

"Honor! Honor Prescott!"

Honor turned toward the sound of the voice calling out her name. She gasped. Was she seeing things?

Joshua was riding Blaze at a full gallop down Jarvis Street and he was heading straight toward her.

Chapter Fourteen

Joshua pulled gently on the reins as he spotted Honor standing next to Ruby outside town hall. There was no mistaking the heart-shaped face and the waves of chestnut hair cascading over her shoulders. She had a pretty pink hat perched on her head.

"Whoa, Blaze." A ripple went through the crowd as they spotted him. People began to whisper Joshua's name and point in his direction. He let out a sigh. Once again, he was the talk of the town. Everyone was gawking at him. Even Hazel was giving him a strange look.

He dismounted from Blaze, then turned toward Honor, who was gazing at him with a shocked expression on her face.

"Joshua! What are you doing here?" Honor asked.

A sudden case of nerves struck him. Did he have the strength to follow through with this? What if she just laughed in his face? What if he was wrong about her returning his tender feelings?

Go big or go home. He had come too far to turn back now. It was time to lay it all on the line.

All of a sudden, Jasper appeared at Honor's side.

"What's with all the dramatics, Ransom?" Jasper barked. "Did you show up here to rub our noses in your victory? We get it. You won. You're about to turn Bud's legacy into a dude ranch. Congratulations."

Joshua swung his gaze toward Honor. "I'm only here for one reason, Mayor Prescott. I need to say something to your granddaughter and it's important. If it's all the same to you, I'd like to speak my piece without being interrupted."

"Oh, brother," Jasper muttered. "Here we go again."

"Hopefully it won't take long," Joshua said with a plucky grin. He turned back around to face Honor. She had been watching and listening intently.

"I came back to Love in order to honor my grandfather. But along the way, something remarkable happened. I fell back in love with you, Honor. Matter of fact, I'm not sure I ever stopped loving you."

Jasper stomped his foot in the snow. "Do we have to listen to this nonsense?"

"Pipe down, Jasper," Boone said in a voice that meant business.

Jasper, muttering under his breath, took a few steps back. He glared at Boone.

"Keep talking, Joshua," Hazel implored him. "Just ignore Jasper's claptrap. We're all ears."

Joshua sent her a smile of gratitude. "Six years ago, I knew without a shadow of a doubt I wanted you to be my wife. There was no question in my mind we were meant to be. I would have joyfully walked down the aisle with you. I was ready to pledge forever to you. But life intruded on our plans."

"Is that a genteel way of saying you set fire to the church?" Jasper barked.

"If you don't hush I'm going to stick you in a snow-bank," Hazel said, jabbing Jasper in the side. He let out a howl.

"I've spent the past six years spinning my wheels and trying to rebuild my life. I've never managed to find anyone who makes me feel even a fraction of what you do. What I should have told you a long time ago is that we got it right the first time around. We knew we were destined to be together. Even at that tender age we knew our hearts." He moved closer to Honor and pulled her toward him.

"In case you didn't hear me earlier, I love you, Honor. I'm head over heels, crazily, helplessly in love with you."

"Oh, Joshua," Honor said, tears flowing down her cheeks.

"Please don't cry," Joshua begged, reaching out and swiping her tears away with his fingers.

"I—I'm just so happy. Hearing you say those words is a healing balm to my soul."

"God led me back home. He led me straight to you. And Bud…I think he knew that by leaving the ranch to me it would cause me to remember all the things I loved about living here. That's what he wanted, Honor. I'm certain of it."

"But you're selling Bud's property to a developer," Dwight Lewis, town treasurer, said in a scandalized voice. "Do you expect Honor to be okay with that? She'll never turn her back on her hometown."

Joshua turned toward Dwight. "Actually I'm not selling to the Alloy Corporation, Dwight. I'm keeping the ranch. Those developers are going to have to find another town to target. They're not getting Ransom land. Not on my watch!"

"Are you serious?" Honor asked, looking up at Joshua with tears pooling in her eyes. "When did this happen? I thought it was a done deal."

Joshua reached out and cupped Honor's chin in his hand. "In my heart it was never a done deal. With each and every day I began to fall in love all over again, not just with you, but with this town and the Diamond R. I can't imagine a better place to raise Violet. She'll be happy here. And hopefully, so will we."

Honor threw her arms around Joshua. "I love you, too, Joshua. I always have."

He leaned down and pressed a kiss against her lips. For a moment it seemed as if they weren't standing in front of a crowd in the middle of Jarvis Street with snow falling all around them. To Joshua, it felt as if it was only the two of them.

"That's enough smooching," Jasper barked.

Hazel raised a tissue to her nose and blew loudly. "I haven't seen anything this romantic since our wedding," she said, sniffing back tears.

"What about Theo?" Honor asked him. "I know how much he wanted to sell to the Alloy Corporation."

"Theo knows how much Joshua sacrificed for him in the past." Theo had made his way toward them. He was standing a few feet away from them with Violet in his arms. "I pretty much owe him everything. Joshua took the blame for the church fire when I was the one responsible. I wish I'd been more courageous at the time." He turned toward the townsfolk. "I want to briefly explain what happened. I set the fire by accident. It was stupid and irresponsible, but not deliberate. Running away from the scene was cowardly." He shook his head. "Joshua was with me at the time, but he didn't have anything to do with starting the fire. Because I was in the army, he wanted to make sure my future was intact, even though his own was compromised because of it. He showed me such grace."

"Such an incredible act of brotherly love," Honor said, squeezing Joshua's hand.

Joshua clapped Theo on the back. "Theo wanted to give me something to show his unconditional love for me. He's giving me the Diamond R."

Theo nodded at him. "Unconditional love. That's what you gave me when you shielded me from responsibility for the fire. It was the most unselfish act I'd ever known. So it's my turn to be altruistic."

"You're giving him controlling interest in the ranch?" Boone asked.

Theo grinned. "Bud's will didn't just name myself and Joshua. It mentioned Violet as well. So, to my way of thinking, Bud wanted Violet to have a say in things. Now she can grow up on the ranch and enjoy the sort of childhood we experienced. I know Joshua would have sold if I pressed it, but it wasn't the right thing to do. Bud just wanted us to sort it out on our own. He had faith in us that we would make the right decision."

"The bottom line is, the Diamond R Ranch is staying in the Ransom family," Joshua announced. "No one's going to be opening a tacky dude ranch on Ransom land."

"Or anywhere else in Love!" Jasper shouted. He raised his fist in the air in a triumphant gesture.

A thunderous clapping rang out. No one was cheering louder than Honor. Joshua loved the transformation on her face. She was radiating joy like a beacon. Jasper stepped forward, quickly followed by Boone and Hazel. Jasper strode over to Joshua and stuck out his hand.

"You've done a good thing, son. I'm proud to shake your hand," Jasper said, grinning at Joshua as if they were best buddies.

"Thank you, Mayor," Joshua said, feeling overjoyed at the notion that Jasper was thawing toward him.

"What's with the mayor nonsense? Call me Jasper." He wiggled his eyebrows. "After all, it sounds like you might be getting hitched to my precious grandbaby."

Honor cried out and covered her face.

"Don't embarrass her!" Hazel scolded, rolling her eyes toward the heavens. "You're about as subtle as a sledgehammer."

Boone stepped forward. He looked Joshua up and down. "It seems I may have been wrong about you. Back in the day, you were a real troublemaker."

Joshua looked Boone straight in the eye. "You're right. I caused a lot of mayhem in this town."

"I appreciate a man who can admit his mistakes and change for the better. What you did for Theo was selfless. I probably would have done the same thing myself," Boone acknowledged.

Relief flooded him. He couldn't believe how this night was turning out. Boone—who had once been his harshest critic—was offering him an olive branch. And he would happily accept it. It brought him one step closer to being with Honor for the long haul.

"Thanks, Boone. Your goodwill means the world to me."

Boone reached out and shook Joshua's hand. Honor

stood beside them, awash in tears. Ruby stood next to her wiping at her eyes. Everyone seemed to be giving in to sentimentality.

Hazel blinked away tears. She cleared her throat. "Let's all head over to the Moose for a celebratory round of espressos and hot chocolates. I'm liable to turn into a pile of mush if I stick around here any longer."

"That's the best idea I've heard all day," Cameron said, placing his arm around Hazel's waist.

Ruby held up her cell phone. "Let me call Liam. He and Aidan can meet us over there since it's not a school night."

"I'll take Violet home so the two of you can celebrate," Theo said. "By the way, I'm really happy for you." He winked at Honor. "I told you he was a good man."

"Thanks, Theo. For everything," Honor gushed. Her eyes were shining brightly and she couldn't seem to stop smiling. "I'm not sure any of this would have happened without you."

"I don't deserve any credit. Just be happy," Theo said.

Honor leaned up and pressed a kiss on Theo's cheek.

As soon as Theo and Violet walked off toward Bud's truck, Honor turned toward Joshua. She had a sheepish expression on her face. "Sorry about Jasper. He shoots from the hip whenever he opens his mouth."

"He's growing on me by leaps and bounds," Joshua said in a teasing tone.

"Jasper does have that effect on people," Honor said with a giggle.

Joshua reached out and pulled Honor toward him.

His hands were on either side of her waist. He was looking deeply into her eyes. All he could see in their depths was love and contentment. It was amazing how quickly things could turn around. With love, hope and faith anything was possible.

He traced her lips with his fingertip. "I want to put down roots right here in Love. With you, Honor. And Violet. I think that's what Bud wanted. He was a pretty romantic guy. One who believed in true love conquering all."

"I have the feeling he's looking down on us and grinning like crazy. I'm proud of you, Joshua. Selling the ranch would have given you and Theo a big payday."

"As long as I have your love, I'll be rich in all the ways that matter most."

She reached up and placed her arms around his neck. They were gazing into each other's eyes. "I can't wait to see what the future holds for us."

"Nothing but blue skies, from this point forward," Joshua said, his words ringing out as a promise for the future.

Honor galloped on Lola across the wide expanse of Ransom land as the wind whipped across her face and hair. March had come in like a lion with a big snowstorm that had wreaked havoc on the small town of Love. After days of being snowbound, the townsfolk were all coming out of hibernation. Honor and Joshua were celebrating their freedom by riding across the Diamond R property.

Joshua was right behind her on Blaze. Honor pulled on Lola's reins and brought the horse to a stop near a stream. She dismounted Lola and led her over toward the partially thawed water. Soon, Joshua joined her. He patted Blaze, murmuring words of praise as he led her to drink.

"Look at all of this beautiful land," Honor said, spreading her arms wide as she whirled around with her face upturned to the sky.

"It stretches out for as far as the eye can see," Joshua said in a voice filled with awe. "Bud created a lasting legacy for his family."

"He was one in a million. A true pioneer." Honor smiled at Joshua. "Thank you for coming back home."

"It's where I belong. God led me straight back to you. And to this amazing town."

"You're a real-life hero. I think the residents are going to put up a statue in your honor since you decided not to sell the Diamond R. You earned everyone's undying devotion. And respect." Honor could hear the pride ringing out in her voice. The man she loved was an amazing human being.

Joshua chuckled. "Let's just say I'm most relieved to find myself in Jasper's good graces. Being on his bad side wasn't pleasant." He scrunched up his face, which made Honor chuckle.

"And my brothers have given us their blessing," she said, blinking away tears. It had always been important to her to know that Liam, Boone and Cameron approved of the man she intended to spend the rest of her days with. They had all rallied around Joshua in the aftermath of the town council meeting where he'd announced his plans to keep the Diamond R Ranch in the family.

He let out a low whistle. "I almost can't believe it. They've been very gracious to me."

"As they should be," Honor teased. "You're all kinds of wonderful."

"You're not so bad yourself," Joshua said.

She shook her head. Sometimes she couldn't believe how beautifully everything had worked out. Right before the town council meeting Honor had been at her lowest point. It had been nearly impossible to hold on to hope.

"Our path has been anything but smooth," she said.

"True. But the beauty of our situation is that our love never died. Not really. I never stopped loving you, Honor."

She looked up at him, her heart brimming with joy. "It feels as if I've always loved you."

He ran a hand across her face. "I hope you always will."

"After everything we've been through, I can't imagine not loving you." She grinned at him. "Joshua. I have something important to ask you."

"You can ask me anything."

Give me courage, Lord, she prayed. *I want a future with Joshua and Violet more than anything else in this world. I want to spend the rest of my life loving and being loved by them.*

"A little more than six years ago you proposed to me. You said that despite our age and the lack of support from my family, we could withstand anything and everything life threw in our direction. Unfortunately, we couldn't live up to that promise we made to one another." She reached for Joshua's hands and squeezed hard. "I want to ask you, Joshua Ransom, to marry me.

We're six years older and wiser now. And we have the full and unwavering support of our families. I want to be your wife. Through good times and bad. And I want to be Violet's mother. I'll be there for her come what may. Through the terrible twos, potty training, the teen years and her first romance. I can't offer you perfection, but I won't ever forsake either one of you, Joshua. Not ever." Tears were streaming down her face and Honor didn't bother wiping them away. She wasn't hiding her feelings anymore. This man was who she wanted to grow old with and shelter from the storms of life. It would be her privilege to be his wife.

"Honor, marrying you would be the supreme honor of my life. I wanted you to be my wife six years ago. That hasn't changed in all this time. I still want you. It would make me the happiest man in all of Alaska to be your husband."

He dug in his pocket and pulled out a shiny diamond solitaire ring. Honor gasped. She covered her mouth with her hands.

"I guess you recognize it. So many times over the years I was tempted to throw it into the river." He shook his head. "I couldn't even think about us because it hurt too badly to go down that road. But something made me hold on to this ring. I couldn't let go of what it represented. When I bought it, I didn't have a whole lot of money to spend on it. But when I gave it to you, it was as if I'd given you the sun, moon and the stars. You didn't care that it wasn't the biggest or the brightest. Because you loved me." He held it out to her. "This ring signifies the most wondrous love I've ever known. Or ever will know."

"Oh, Joshua. It's still the most beautiful ring I've ever seen," she exclaimed.

"Honor, will you wear my ring? Again? And this time promise never to take it off. Will you marry me?" Joshua asked.

Honor began laughing through her tears. "Hey! No fair. I asked you first. You never gave me an answer."

Joshua reached for her hand and slid the ring onto her finger. "This is my answer. Yes, Honor. I'll marry you. Anytime. Anyplace. Anywhere."

Honor threw herself against Joshua's chest and wrapped her arms around his neck. He placed his hands on either side of her waist and whirled her around. Honor let out a squeal of delight and hung on for dear life. Finally, after all these years, they were getting married. And she would be a mother to Violet. All of her dreams were coming to fruition. She was incredibly blessed.

She had never imagined Joshua's return to Love would result in their falling in love all over again. Their reunion had been given a push in the right direction by the good Lord above. She just knew it!

All things were possible with love, truth and faith. She truly believed it now. She and Joshua had been through the fire and come through the ashes to form something stronger than they had ever imagined. And there was no force on earth that they would ever allow to separate them again.

Like their beloved hometown, their love would endure.

Epilogue

Joshua stood at the front of the church dressed in a dark suit and tie. His wedding day had arrived. Hazel had placed a red carnation in his lapel to match the bridesmaids' flowers. The way he saw it, he was a simple man who finally was getting his heart's desire—marrying the woman of his dreams. After all this time, they were making it official. Mr. and Mrs. Joshua Ransom.

He shifted from one foot to the other as nerves began to grab ahold of him. His palms began to moisten.

"Are you okay?" Theo asked, nudging him in the side. "You're fidgeting quite a bit."

"I think so. I mean, yes, of course I am. It's just that I forgot something important." Joshua fumbled with his words. He turned toward his brother. "I need to go talk to Honor."

Theo's eyes bulged. "Now? Are you serious?"

"Don't worry. I'll be right back," Joshua said, walking quickly toward the back of the church, past all the guests who were seated in the pews and staring at him with wide eyes. People began whispering and pointing.

As he headed toward the changing room where the bridal party was gathered, Hazel cut him off at the pass.

"Joshua! What are you doing back here?" Hazel asked. "The wedding is about to start." She frowned at him. "You're not having second thoughts, are you?"

He leaned down and kissed Hazel on the cheek. "Of course I'm not. Marrying Honor is all I've ever wanted. I just need to say something to her before we exchange our vows."

Hazel began fanning herself with her hand. "Praise the Lord. You just scared the life out of me. An image flashed in my head of all the Prescott men running you out of town on a rail."

Joshua grinned. He could actually laugh at the idea of it, now that things had been smoothed over between him and Honor's family. They had finally shown him grace and acceptance. Hopefully, they would forge a good relationship in the years to come.

"There won't be any drama today, Hazel. I'm marrying the woman of my dreams. I just need for Honor to stand on the other side of the door. If you open it a crack I can talk to her from the other side without seeing her."

Hazel looked at him skeptically. "Okay. I'll pass it on to her." A few minutes later Hazel waved him toward the partially opened door. "She's standing right behind the door. Make it quick, partner. There's a whole church full of people waiting with bated breath for this wedding to start." She winked at him. "After all, it's been six years in the making." Hazel patted him on the shoulder as she walked past him down the hall.

Joshua walked toward the door and faced away from

it. He reached out his arm through the opening and said, "Honor. Are you there? I'd like us to pray before Pastor Jack marries us."

"I'm here, my love." He felt Honor's hand join with his own. She squeezed his hand and he heard her from the other side of the door. "Of course I'll pray with you, Joshua."

Joshua smiled. He closed his eyes and began to pray out loud. "Lord. Thank You for giving us this day and for bringing us back together. You have brought us forgiveness, healing and restoration. Without You I don't think we would have found our way back to each other. Your love humbles us. Please bless our marriage with kindness and faith and devotion. If we make mistakes, give us the grace to forgive one another. And if we ever face any health challenges, may the stronger one hold the other one up. If You see fit, please allow us to grow our family, so that Violet can be a loving big sister and we can cherish more children. And can You please watch over the child we lost until we are all reunited one day. Amen."

"Amen." Honor's voice resonated from the other side.

He squeezed her hand. "Thank you for praying with me."

"Thank you, Joshua. For being the type of man who wanted to pray with me before you greet me at the altar."

Joshua let go of her hand. "I'll see you in a few minutes."

Ten minutes later the wedding march was playing and Ruby, Grace, Paige and Sophie were walking down the aisle scattering rose petals. Aidan followed closely behind them carrying a pillow as the ring bearer. Suddenly, Honor was walking down the aisle toward him. His heart caught in his throat. He could barely catch a breath. She was radiantly beautiful.

Honor was walking down the aisle, with Jasper by her side. She was dressed in a long-sleeved ivory gown with a sweetheart neckline and a veil trailing past her shoulders. There were shiny rhinestones on the bodice of her dress. She came toward him with a big smile on her face. Her expression radiated love.

"I'm handing over to you our Prescott princess," Jasper said, sniffing back tears. "She's the very best of us, Joshua. Protect her. Love her. Give her a pair of strong arms to hold her when the world gets tough."

Joshua looked Jasper straight in the eye, then shook his hand. "I will always love and honor her, Jasper. I promise."

Jasper was beaming. "You're part of our family now, Joshua. An honorary Prescott."

"I never thought I'd hear you say that," Joshua teased, gaining a chorus of laughter from the guests. "I'm grateful we can be a family."

Jasper leaned over and kissed Honor on the cheek. He pulled a handkerchief out of his jacket pocket and began wiping his eyes with it. He walked over to the front pew and sat down with Hazel and Violet.

Violet reached out and yanked on Jasper's beard. He let out a slight yelp. The sound of Hazel's laughter rang out.

Pastor Jack began to speak. "Of all the couples I've married, I think the two of you make me feel the most hopeful. Your love endured a lot of trials. You faced a lot of obstacles. You climbed mountains in order to be together. Your love won't be shaken. It's a mighty thing indeed."

"You may now recite your vows," Pastor Jack intoned.

Joshua cleared his throat. "You were my first love, Honor. And now you're my forever love."

She reached for his hand. "You've been imprinted on my soul since I was a teenager. That hasn't changed one iota. I'll be by your side, come what may. That's my solemn promise to you."

After Pastor Jack declared them as husband and wife, Joshua leaned down and placed a tender kiss on Honor's lips. The guests began to clap enthusiastically.

Hazel handed Violet over to Joshua, who held her tightly against his chest with one hand and gripped Honor's hand with the other.

As they walked out of the church, a shower of flower petals rained down on them. The sky was shining beautifully. The blue skies above were the color of a robin's egg and cloudless.

Honor looked around her. Joy hummed and pulsed in the air. Operation Love had surely blessed this town. Love was all around her. Boone, Grace and baby Eva. Cameron, Paige and Emma. Liam, Ruby and Aidan. Jasper stood hand in hand with Hazel, who was looking up at him with adoration. Declan had his arms around a heavily pregnant Annie. Finn, Maggie and Oliver were smiling and laughing. Sophie and Noah still were acting like newlyweds and seemed head over heels for each other.

Honor had always believed in happy endings. She had hers now. There wasn't a single doubt in her mind that she, Joshua and Violet would live happily-ever-after. She would continue her work at the wildlife center and Joshua would be running the Diamond R Ranch—their new home. Bud's legacy would live on and thrive.

This was it. She had found her happy place and all the things she had never thought were quite possible. Joshua squeezed her hand then brought it up to his lips and placed a kiss on it. "Are you ready, my love?" he asked, resting Violet on his hip. Dressed in a lilac dress with a big bow in front, she looked adorable.

"Yes, Joshua. I've been waiting for this moment all of my life." She reached out and began to pat Violet's back in a soothing manner. "God has blessed us both in abundance."

"He has," Joshua said. "He gave me redemption and an opportunity to win back the love of my life."

Honor reached up and pressed a kiss on her husband's lips. "He sent you back to me. That was the best gift of all. God is good!"

"All the time," Joshua said in a voice filled with conviction.

This time around Honor and Joshua weren't going to falter when hard times came knocking. They were going to fight for their marriage and bask in their love story. There was a quiet strength in knowing their love was an enduring one. Their union was strong enough to conquer any storms. With an abundance of love, anything was possible.

* * * * *

*If you enjoyed this book, look for the other books
in the ALASKAN GROOMS series:*

*AN ALASKAN WEDDING
ALASKAN REUNION
A MATCH MADE IN ALASKA
REUNITED AT CHRISTMAS
HIS SECRET ALASKAN HEIRESS
AN ALASKAN CHRISTMAS*

Available now from Love Inspired!

Find more great reads at www.LoveInspired.com

Dear Reader,

Thank you for joining me on this Alaskan journey. Writing this Alaskan Grooms series has been a romance writer's dream. I've had so much fun creating this Alaska-based series. The town of Love is filled with some very special characters. A sense of community ties them all together. Honor and Joshua are a fitting couple to end this series. They are two wonderful people who have been gifted with a second chance at love. Having fallen in love as teenagers, then ending an engagement at eighteen, they have truly earned their happy ending. Their love has endured. It grew and blossomed the second time around. Neither one of them had ever truly given up on each other. Their happy ending is a sweet reward.

Writing for the Love Inspired line is an honor. I feel very blessed to have my dream job. What's better than working in my pajamas? I enjoy hearing from readers however you may choose to contact me. I can be reached by email at *scalhoune@gmail.com* or at bellecalhoune.com. If you're on Facebook, please stop by my Author Belle Calhoune page.

Blessings,
Belle

Get 2 Free Books,
Plus 2 Free Gifts—
just for trying the
Reader Service!

Ten years ago, Jeremiah Weaver left his Amish community to become a navy SEAL. Now that he's back, can he convince the woman he left behind—widow and mother of two Ava Jane Graber—that he's here to stay?

Read on for a sneak preview of
THEIR AMISH REUNION,
by **Lenora Worth**,
available April 2018 from Love Inspired!

"What are you doing here, Jeremiah?"

"I didn't want you to see me yet," he tried to explain.

"Too late." She adjusted her *kapp* with shaking hands. "I need to go."

"Please, don't," he said. "I'm not going to bother you. I…I saw you and I didn't have time to—"

"To leave again?" she asked, her tone full of more venom than he could ever imagine coming from such a sweet soul.

"I'm not leaving," he said. "I've come back to Campton Creek to help my family. But I had planned on coming to pay you and Jacob a visit, to let you know that…I understand how things are. You're married—"

"I'm a widow now," she blurted, two bright spots forming on her cheeks. "I have to get my children home."

Kneeling, she tried to pick up her groceries, but his hand on her arm stopped her. Jeremiah took the torn bag and placed the thread, spices and canned goods inside the bottom, the feel of sticky honey on his fingers merging with the memory of her dainty arm. But the shock of her words made him numb with regret.

I'm a widow now.

"I'm sorry," Jeremiah said in a whisper. "Beth never told me."

"You couldn't be reached."

Ah, so Beth had tried but he'd been on a mission.

"I wish I'd known. I'm so sorry."

Ava Jane kept her eyes downcast while she tried to gather the rest of her groceries and toss them into the torn bag.

"Here you go," he said, while her news echoed through his mind. "I'll go inside and get something to clean the honey."

Their eyes met as his hand brushed over hers.

A rush of deep longing shot through her eyes, jagged and fractured, and hit Jeremiah straight in his heart.

Ava Jane recoiled and stood. *"Denke."*

Then she turned and hurried toward the buggy. Just before she got inside, she pivoted back to give him one last glaring appraisal. "I wonder why you came back at all."

He watched as she got into the buggy and sat for a moment. Without a backward glance, Ava Jane held her head high. Then Jeremiah asked for a wet mop to clean the stains from the sidewalk. He only wished he could clean away the stains inside of his heart.

And just like her, he wondered why he'd returned to Campton Creek.

Don't miss
THEIR AMISH REUNION by Lenora Worth,
available April 2018 wherever
Love Inspired® books and ebooks are sold.

www.LoveInspired.com

Looking for inspiration in tales
of hope, faith and heartfelt romance?

Check out **Love Inspired**® and
Love Inspired® **Suspense** books!

New books available every month!

Love Inspired®

LIGENRE2018

SPECIAL EXCERPT FROM

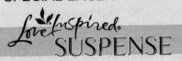
Love Inspired
SUSPENSE

*A serial killer is on the loose on a military base—
can the Military K-9 Unit track him down?*

Read on for a sneak preview of
MISSION TO PROTECT *by* Terri Reed,
the first book in the brand-new
MILITARY K-9 UNIT *miniseries,*
available April 2018 from Love Inspired Suspense!

Staff Sergeant Felicity Monroe jerked awake to the fading sound of her own scream echoing through her head. Sweat drenched her nightshirt. The pounding of her heart hurt in her chest, making bile rise to burn her throat. Darkness surrounded her.

Where was she? Fear locked on and wouldn't let go. Panic fluttered at the edge of her mind.

Her breathing slowed. She wiped at the wet tears on her cheeks and shook away the fear and panic.

She filled her lungs with several deep breaths and sought the clock across the room on the dresser.

The clock's red glow was blocked by the silhouette of a person looming at the end of her bed.

Someone was in her room!

Full-fledged panic jackknifed through her, jolting her system into action. She rolled to the side of the bed and landed soundlessly on the floor. With one hand, she reached for the switch on the bedside table lamp while her other hand reached for the baseball bat she kept under the bed.

Holding the bat up with her right hand, she flicked on the light. A warm glow dispelled the shadows and revealed she was alone. Or was she?

She searched the house, turning on every light. No one was there.

She frowned and worked to calm her racing pulse.

Back in her bedroom, her gaze landed on the clock. Wait a minute. It was turned to face the wall. A shiver of unease racked her body. The red numbers had been facing the bed when she'd retired last night. She was convinced of it.

And her dresser drawers were slightly open. She peeked inside. Her clothes were mussed as if someone had rummaged through them.

What was going on?

Noises outside the bedroom window startled her. It was too early for most people to be up on a Sunday morning. She pushed aside the room-darkening curtain. The first faint rays of sunlight marched over the Texas horizon with hues of gold, orange and pink.

And provided enough light for Felicity to see a parade of dogs running loose along Base Boulevard. It could only be the dogs from the K-9 training center.

Stunned, her stomach clenched. Someone had literally let the dogs out. All of them, by the looks of it.

Don't miss
MISSION TO PROTECT by Terri Reed,
available April 2018 wherever
Love Inspired® Suspense books and ebooks are sold.

www.LoveInspired.com

Inspirational Romance to Warm Your Heart and Soul

Join our social communities to connect
with other readers who share your love!

Sign up for the Love Inspired newsletter
at **www.LoveInspired.com** to be the
first to find out about upcoming titles,
special promotions and exclusive content.

CONNECT WITH US AT:

Harlequin.com/Community

 Facebook.com/LoveInspiredBooks

 Twitter.com/LoveInspiredBks

LISOCIAL2017